PRAISE FOR STEVEN PAJAK

"Steven Pajak delivers another devilishly dark tale of dabbling in the occult and the demonic entities daring you to open a doorway. In the hands of a lesser author, this could be another color-by-numbers cautionary tale, but Pajak takes his time, letting you settle in and cozy up to the characters before literally splitting the seams of existence...and your peace of mind."

— NICK ROBERTS, AUTHOR OF MEAN SPIRITED AND THE EXORCIST'S HOUSE

"The Devil's Doorway is one of those books that instantly feels made for the silver screen. Pajak effortlessly delivers a tight plot, realistic and enjoyable characters, and a high-stakes plot sure to unnerve even the most seasoned horror reader. Not a read I'll soon forget."

— MEGAN STOCKTON, AUTHOR OF LOVELY, DARK & DEEP AND BLUEJAY

"Pajak writes with such heart and passion it's impossible not to root for his characters. Human connection and purpose, courage in the face of hopelessness, and selfless love are explored against a hellish backdrop of nightmare-fuel. From the first few pages I knew I was in for a great time with this book - it takes a lot to scare me, and I had a spooky blast with this book!"

— MJ MARS AUTHOR OF THE SUFFERING AND WE'VE ALREADY GONE TOO FAR

THE DEVIL'S DOORWAY

THE DEVIL'S DOORWAY

STEVEN PAJAK

INSIDIOUS PRESS

The Devil's Doorway
Steven Pajak

Published by Lakefront Terror Press

Copyright © 2024 by Steven Pajak
Cover art by Lance Dale
Interior art by Jaime Stearns

All rights reserved.

This book or any portion thereof may not be reproduced or used in any manner whatsoever without the express written permission of the publisher, except for the use of brief quotations in a book review. This is a work of fiction. Names, characters, businesses, places, events, and incidents are either the products of the author's imagination or used in a fictitious manner. Any resemblance to actual persons, living or dead, or actual events is purely coincidental.

Printed in the United States of America

Trade Hardcover: 978-1-966701-03-3

CONTENTS

PART ONE
Prologue (The Shadow Man Cometh) — 3
The Threshold of Darkness — 17
Nightmares and Warnings — 27
A Twist of Fate — 45
A Gathering Darkness — 61
The Crow's Omen — 71
A Grim Prognosis — 83
A Canvas of Horrors — 93

PART TWO
Requiem for Walter — 105
In Dreams, A Reckoning — 119
The Mysterious Mourner — 129
Nightmare Manifestation — 139
Shattering Circle — 155

PART THREE
A Portrait of Agony — 167
Into the Abyss — 175
The Devil's Bargain — 183
Tiqua's Gambit — 191
The Rabbit Hole's End — 197
Epilogue — 207

About the Author — 215
Also by Steven Pajak — 217

"The mind is its own place, and in itself can make a heaven of hell, a hell of heaven."

— JOHN MILTON, PARADISE LOST

PART ONE

PROLOGUE (THE SHADOW MAN COMETH)

Walter sat at the kitchen table, the pale white scented candle flickering with each labored exhale. The almond-vanilla aroma, Eleanor's favorite, swirled around him in wisps of warmth and painful recollection. He bought the candles in bulk, lighting one each night without fail as he surrendered to the relentless undertow of memories of his beloved wife, even two years after her passing.

Eleanor had been his constant, his unwavering lodestar for nearly six decades of life shared in tandem. Best friends from the tender age of five, when the world was a wondrous uncertainty to be experienced through the kaleidoscope vision of youth. High school sweethearts stumbling with bravery into the throes of first love, a bond reinforced over aimless summers and shared adolescent dreams. Until finally husband and wife on the precipice of adulthood, taking that fateful leap together in partnership the moment they received their minted diplomas.

She was the cornerstone of his existence, the tremulous yet mighty foundation upon which every piece of the person he had become had been constructed, hewn from her passionate spirit and steadfast devotion over the passing decades. Now her absence gnawed ever deeper, a gaping, soul-crushing void that consumed him by incremental degrees.

Six months ago, at Kate's gentle insistence, Walter had reluctantly begun seeing a grief counselor. The counselor, recognizing the depths of Walter's sorrow, suggested painting as a way to channel his overwhelming emotions. It was a lifeline Walter grasped desperately, pouring his heartache onto canvas, desperately trying to recreate the warmth and laughter of cherished moments with Eleanor. But even after countless scenes based on his fondest memories of shared experiences with Eleanor, each brushstroke was a painful echo of happier times, the gnawing void within him remained, a black hole devouring his heart.

Eventually, the thought of reaching out to Eleanor through a medium had crept into Walter's mind like a wisp of smoke, a fleeting notion that gradually solidified into a desperate hope. He was a man of logic and reason, a pragmatic soul who had never truly embraced the concept of spirits or the ethereal realm of the afterlife. Church attendance had been a dutiful gesture, a concession to appease his devout wife, rather than a reflection of his own beliefs. But now, the yearning to connect with his beloved Eleanor, to bridge the chasm that separated them, had become a consuming obsession, a relentless siren song echoing in the depths of his despair.

He needed to know, with every fiber of his being, that she was at peace, that her spirit was free from pain and sorrow. He ached to express the boundless love he held for her, the profound impact she had made on his life. These unspoken words gnawed at him, a tormenting chorus whispering in the shadows, fueling a desperate need for closure, for one final, bittersweet connection.

The sharp rap on the door jolted him back to the present. 10 PM on the dot—Tiqua was always punctual. Muscles aching from an hour hunched over the table lost in a bittersweet haze of memory, Walter blew out the flickering candle and made his way to the door.

Tiqua Lovett stood on the threshold, a wisp of a figure barely reaching Walter's shoulder, her boyish pixie cut and dark-framed glasses perched on a delicate nose were an absolute contrast to her pale complexion. The porch light washed over her, making her appear even younger than her early thirties, more akin to a curious adolescent than the matronly mystic he'd envisioned when he first stepped into her dimly lit shop months ago. Her youth had given him pause then, but desperation had ultimately triumphed over doubt.

"Hello, Walter," she greeted, fidgeting on the stoop.

"Come in." He closed the door behind them and ushered her past the kitchen. "Let's go upstairs."

Tiqua trailed behind him through the hushed house, the darkness pressing in around them as they ascended the stairs to the converted bedroom studio. Walter moved with the unerring familiarity of a blind man, navigating the cluttered studio effortlessly. He lit a candle at his desk, casting flickering shadows that danced and twisted on the walls. With a silent gesture, he invited her to take a seat.

The air hung heavy with the scent of almond-vanilla, an overlay to the underlying metallic tang that prickled at the back of Tiqua's throat. The worn surface of the desk was dominated by an ornate Ouija board, its planchette resting ominously like a trapped insect, an invitation to a spectral dialogue.

Tiqua faltered at the sight of the spirit board, lifting her tarot deck. "Walter, you know I work with the cards."

"I know," he replied impatiently, "but we've tried that route three times already without success."

She sighed. "I warned you connecting isn't guaranteed. If the spirits aren't ready or willing, we can't force it."

"I get that, I really do, but I believe the board offers a more direct line. I've been researching," Walter pressed, fingertips grazing the planchette.

Frowning, Tiqua set her cards aside. "Ouija boards are dangerous, Walter. You're opening a portal you might not be able to close. Tarot lets me retain control in a way the board doesn't."

"But you have to interpret the cards. I want to hear directly from Eleanor," he countered, voice strained.

"I don't like this," she muttered uneasily.

Walter's eyes narrowed. "Do you actually want to help me or have you just been scamming me all along?"

Tiqua recoiled as if slapped, her voice rising when she asked, "Is that what you think? That I'm conning you? I've done everything possible to guide you safely through this. If I was scamming you, I'd just tell you whatever you want to hear and take your money, no questions asked!"

Raising placating hands, Walter apologized. "I'm sorry, I didn't mean it like that. I'm just...so damn frustrated. I feel like we're on the cusp of reaching her..."

The raw ache in his voice softened Tiqua's anger, but trepidation still clouded her features as she eyed the board. After a tense moment, she turned to him gravely.

"I'll do this, but you have to swear you'll follow my lead. The second I say stop, we stop. No arguing. Deal?"

At his solemn nod, she sighed heavily. "All right then. Let's see what the spirits have to say."

Taking a fortifying breath, Tiqua placed the planchette on the board, fingers poised above its surface. "Put your hands on it with me. Lightly. We'll let the spirits steer."

Walter obeyed, their fingers brushing as they made contact. Tiqua shut her eyes, concentrating.

"Eleanor, we reach out to you now, from the living to the dead. If you're here, please make yourself known. Guide our hands and speak through this vessel."

A heavy silence settled over the room as Tiqua closed her eyes, her breathing slowing as she reached for a connection. Minutes ticked by, each one amplifying the tension in the air. She discerned Walter's growing agitation, but she remained steadfast, her senses attuned to any whispers from beyond the veil.

Just as she contemplated breaking the silence again, the planchette quivered to life beneath their fingers. It moved hesitantly at first, then with increasing purpose, its journey across the board tracing a name in the candlelight.

E-L-E-A-N-O-R

Walter's breath hitched in his chest, his voice a hoarse whisper. "Eleanor? Is it truly you?"

Despite her years of experience and carefully cultivated composure, a chill slithered down Tiqua's spine. This was no ordinary unease that accompanied initial contact across the spiritual veil. It was a primal, visceral reaction, the gut-wrenching sensation of being hunted by something ancient and unspeakably evil.

The planchette, as if echoing her dread, confirmed with an unequivocal:

YES

Emotion choked Walter's words, his voice thick with unshed tears. "Eleanor, my love, there's so much I need to say..."

The planchette, as if startled by his outburst, lurched into motion once more, its movements even more frenzied than before.

N-O-T-S-A-F-E

Tiqua's brow furrowed, a flicker of unease crossing her face. "What do you mean by 'not safe,' Eleanor?"

The planchette's movements became even more frenzied, seeking the letters frantically, darting across the board's glossy surface.

D-A-R-K-N-E-S-S-C-O-M-I-N-G

Walter's face drained of color. "Darkness? What darkness?"

Without warning, the planchette rocketed off the board, clattering to the floor. Tiqua recoiled, her heart thumping in her chest. She looked up, her wide eyes locking with Walter's across the table. His face was pale and stricken.

"Walter, we need to stop. Now."

But he was already on his feet, his movements frantic as he snatched the planchette from the floor and slammed it back onto the board. His eyes were wild with desperation.

"No!" he shouted. "Please, Eleanor," he pleaded. "This darkness—what is it? Are you in the darkness, honey?"

A tense silence filled the room before the planchette shuddered back to life. It moved slowly at first, then with gradually increasing speed. Tiqua realized with mounting horror that it was no longer being guided by their hands. It was moving on its own.

H-E-I-S-H-E-R-E

The air grew frigid, the temperature plummeting twenty degrees in just seconds. A shiver racked Tiqua's body, her blood turning to ice in her veins.

"Who, Eleanor? Who is here?"

The planchette vibrated with a frenzied energy, its movements erratic and uncontrolled.

T-H-E-S-H-A-D-O-W-M-A-N

As the final letter spelled out the words, a bone-chilling gust of wind ripped through the room, extinguishing the candle and plunging them into absolute darkness. Tiqua made a mewling sound, her chair scraping against the floor as she scrambled away from the table.

"Walter, stop this right now!"

She fumbled for the light switch, her fingers scrabbling against the wall blindly seeking. Even through the overwhelming terror that gripped her, she sensed it—a malevolent presence seeping into the room, its essence thick and suffocating, hungry for a foothold in their world. They had unwittingly opened a door to something far more sinister than they could have ever imagined.

But Walter was past hearing, eyes blazed with an unhinged fervor in the gloom. "We've made contact! Don't you dare stop now!"

"Move the planchette to 'Goodbye'!" Fear had ripped away the veneer of Tiqua's professional calm, leaving her voice raw and desperate. "We need to end this connection before it's too late!"

A guttural growl reverberated from the depths of the studio, the floorboards trembling beneath them with the force of it. Before Tiqua could even gasp, an unseen force slammed into her, an invisible battering ram that struck her like a freight train.

A shriek tore from her lips as she was flung across the room, stars bursting in her vision as she crashed to the ground. Agony exploded in her shoulder, a white-hot fire that threatened to consume her entirely.

Whimpering, Tiqua pulled herself onto her hands and knees, her head swimming with dizziness. Through blurred vision, she saw Walter bathed in the shadows, his face twisted into a grotesque caricature of both ecstasy and terror.

"Eleanor? Speak to me!"

The very air seethed with putrid energy. It invaded Tiqua's

nostrils, slithered down her throat. Mere feet away, one of Walter's paintings—a faceless woman in a picturesque park—slid from its easel and crumpled to the floor beside her, as if struck by an immense, unseen force.

And then the woman's unfinished face began to writhe and contort on the canvas. Tiqua watched in paralyzed horror as the peach-colored oval warped and twisted, stretching into a nightmarish parody of a human face, its mouth agape in a silent shriek.

With a sound like rending flesh, a seam split down the center of the canvas, jagged edges peeling back to reveal a terrible, pulsating nothingness that could not exist. A darkness blacker than black, yet somehow sentient, oozing greed and cruel intent and a bottomless, fathomless hunger.

The scream that tore from Tiqua's throat was a raw, guttural sound, more animal than human, a primal shriek of pure terror. Ignoring the searing agony in her shoulder, she scrambled to her feet, ripping open the studio door and stumbling blindly down the hallway.

The aged floorboards groaned and creaked under her frantic flight, the wood seeming to warp and twist beneath her as if the very house were convulsing, desperate to expel her like a venomous parasite invader.

Behind her, a nightmarish wail echoed through the house. The hideous, warped sound pierced her eardrums, a sound that defied all sense and reason. She didn't dare turn, didn't even slow, even as the unnatural keen abruptly ceased, leaving a ringing silence that was somehow more terrifying than the scream itself.

Tiqua hit the front door at a dead run, clawing at the knob with hands that shook so violently she could barely turn it. The heavy wood gave with a protesting squeal and she tumbled out into the crisp night, gulping air that seared her lungs but was blessedly, mercifully, free of the putrescent taint that had defiled Walter's house.

Behind her, light blazed from the upstairs studio window, pulsing with a corpse-light glow that made her gorge rise. And beneath that awful brilliance, a new sound reached her —low, chittering, wet. Chewing. Gnawing. Devouring.

On legs that barely supported her weight, Tiqua staggered toward the dented Toyota Camry parked at the curb. Some distant part of her quailed in shame at her cowardice, at abandoning Walter to the horror they'd unleashed.

But this was no mere restless spirit or petulant poltergeist to be subdued with prayers and ritual. This was something else, something older, viler. Something that wore darkness like a second skin and hungered for more than lost souls to slake its appetite.

It took three tries with her slick, trembling fingers to jam the key into the ignition. The anemic sputter of the engine was immediately smothered by an oppressive silence pressing against the car windows, the street, the whole world.

She threw the car into reverse, tires squealing against the pavement as she peeled backward down the block. Once she judged herself far enough away, she slammed the brakes, chest heaving as if she'd just finished a marathon.

The sensible thing would be to keep driving until the nightmare was miles behind in her rearview mirror. But a tattered scrap of conscience stopped her short. With a trembling hand, she fished her cell phone from her jacket, fumbling with the screen until she managed to dial 911.

"I heard screaming," she rasped when the dispatcher answered, the lie like ash on her tongue. "My neighbor... I think he might be hurt." She rattled off Walter's address, then thumbed the end button, letting the phone fall into her lap.

The green glow of the dashboard lights made her drawn features look skeletal. Her reflection in the rearview mirror was that of a woman barely recognizable, eyes glassy and unfocused, tear tracks cutting through the runnels of cheap mascara.

"I'm sorry," she croaked. "God, Walter, I'm so sorry."

But beneath the guilt, beneath the gut-churning shame...there pulsed an ugly sliver of relief. Relief that she was here, and not in that house. Not even the most jaded or veteran medium could have walked away from what she'd just experienced unscathed.

Closing her eyes, she gripped the steering wheel, feeling the car throb around her like the heartbeat of a dying beast. Behind clenched lids, afterimages danced—that awful, hungry dark, the rending canvas, Walter's ecstatic, horrified face limned in sickly light.

And then, the silence. That was perhaps the most terrifying thing of all. Because Tiqua knew, with an instinctual dread that chilled her to the core, that this silence was not merely the absence of sound. It was the bated breath before the predator's lunge. The charged stillness before the final, fatal strike. And she'd just set it loose.

THE THRESHOLD OF DARKNESS

Kate rolled over in bed, fumbling in the darkness for the ringing phone that had startled her awake. Disoriented, she reached out toward the nightstand, her fingers finally closing around the device. She lifted it, squinting against the harsh rectangle of light in the gloom. Her father's name glowed on the screen, and a familiar dread pooled in her stomach—he only called after midnight for emergencies, like when Mom...

Pushing herself into a seated position, back against the headboard and legs crossed in front of her, Kate tapped the Accept icon. Her heartbeat quickened as she pressed the phone to her ear, her voice thick with sleep. "Dad?"

"Kate..." His voice sounded weak and distant, nearly drowned out by static that crackled across the line. It wasn't the usual hiss of a bad connection, but a persistent, organic buzzing, like a swarm of angry flies trapped inside the phone. When Walter spoke again, his words were a strained whisper, barely audible over the interference.

"Katie...you have to..." The sentence fractured, punctuated by buzzing and hisses.

"Dad? Hello?" Kate's voice trembled as she pressed her palm against her other ear, trying to block out the angry drone that seemed to grow louder with each passing second.

"...have...close...door..." he croaked, his voice fading in and out of the incessant buzzing. "...never should...opened..."

"What?" She strained to make out the words, pressing the phone tighter to her ear and the buzzing intensified, a thousand phantom insects burrowing into her skull. "Dad, I can't hear you. Where are you?"

"...door, Katie...CLOSE THE—"

A low, gravelly growl erupted from the receiver, morphing into a bloodcurdling shriek that tore through the night's silence. White-hot pain lanced through Kate's ear, a searing agony that ripped a scream from her throat. Recoiling, she flung the phone away, sending it clattering against the headboard before it settled onto the mattress a few feet from her.

Clamping her hands over her ears, Kate squeezed her eyes shut, but the sound persisted, emanating from the phone in relentless waves. Her face contorted as the steady ringing flooded her inner ear, nausea churning in her gut. Something slick and warm trickled against her left palm, and she slowly lowered her hand, staring in mute horror at the blood staining her skin.

The phone lay silent on the bed, screen dark, yet the muffled ringing continued, as if originating from within the very walls of the room. Kate scrambled out of bed on shaky legs, her vision blurring at the edges as her heart hammered a frantic tattoo against her ribs.

She scanned the room wildly, searching for the source of the phantom noise. The shadows in the corners seemed deeper, darker than usual, pulsing with a malevolent energy. A soft scratching drew her attention to the bedroom door, and she watched, paralyzed with terror, as it creaked open inch by inch.

Beyond the widening gap, pure, inky darkness rippled like oil, oozing over the threshold in a gelatinous tide. Icy tendrils of air snaked around Kate's ankles, sending fresh shudders down her spine.

From the doorway, a raspy voice hissed, chilling her to the marrow. *"You shouldn't have answered..."*

Kate's scream withered in her throat as a tall, shapeless form coalesced in the doorway, the ringing in her ears intensifying to a sanity-shattering whine. Just as the figure lunged forward, a jarring blare cut through the room—

—and Kate jolted upright, a ragged gasp tearing from her lungs as fear's cold sweat prickled her skin. She clutched the sheets with white-knuckled fingers, chest heaving as the remnants of the nightmare slowly dissipated.

"Fuck," she croaked, her voice a shaky rattle in her throat. The phone rang again, startling her badly enough that her hands flew to her chest, trying to contain the wildly galloping heart beneath her ribs.

She snatched the phone from the nightstand on the third ring, her father's name once again glowing on the screen. "Dad?"

"Hello...is this Kate Emerson?" The voice on the other end was unfamiliar, professionally brisk.

"Yes, who is this?" Kate asked, dread crystallizing in her gut.

"I apologize for the late hour. This is Melissa, a nurse at Thorek Memorial Hospital. I'm calling about your father, Walter Emerson. He was brought into the ER a few hours ago—"

"Oh my God, what happened? Is he all right?" Kate interrupted, panic clawing up her throat.

The nurse's tone gentled, but the news remained grim. "I'm sorry to have to tell you this, but Walter was unconscious and unresponsive upon arrival. The doctors are still assessing his condition, but I'm afraid we don't have many answers at the moment. Dr. Phillips was hoping you could come to the hospital as soon as possible..."

"I understand," Melissa said, sympathy threading her words. "When do you think you might be able to get here?"

Kate's gaze darted around the room, landing on the clock's harsh red glow. 2:14 AM. "I don't know. I have to check flights, pack a bag..." She trailed off, the enormity of the situation crashing over her in a suffocating wave.

"Let's do this," the nurse offered. "I'll give you my direct line. Call me once you have your travel details ironed out, and I can update you on any changes in Walter's status. Do you have something to write with?"

"No, hang on." Kate slid out of bed, bare feet slapping against the chilly hardwood as she stumbled to the small desk in the corner. She yanked open the middle drawer, rummaging until she located a stray Post-It pad and pen. "Okay, go ahead."

Melissa rattled off the number, and Kate scribbled it down, the pen nearly tearing through the flimsy paper in her haste. "I'm here until 8 AM, Central time," the nurse said. "If you call after that, ask for Kim. She's the next shift nurse, and she'll have the most current information on your father's condition."

"Thank you," Kate whispered, ending the call and sinking heavily into the desk chair. She stared at the number, the ink blurring as hot tears welled in her eyes. Her mind spun with the overwhelming logistics—booking a flight, packing, notifying her law firm, delegating her caseload. She had no idea how long she'd need to be away. A week? Two? There were trials looming, clients depending on her...

"*...door, Katie...CLOSE THE—*" Her father's fractured warning from the dream echoed in her mind, sending a fresh shudder down her spine.

Trying to shake off the unease coiling in her chest, Kate flipped open her laptop and pulled up a travel site, fingers trembling as she navigated the booking process.

The only available flight was a red eye with an astronomical price tag, but Kate barely blinked as she entered her credit card information. Time was a luxury she couldn't afford. She booked a rental car to pick up at O'Hare, then placed a frantic call to the firm, leaving a rambling voicemail explaining the situation and hastily delegating her most pressing cases to the junior associates.

Exhaustion dragged at her, but adrenaline kept her moving as she threw clothes and toiletries into a carry-on weekender bag. Each completed task chipped away at the dread calcifying in her veins, slowly replacing it with steely resolve. An hour later, bag in hand and heart lodged somewhere in her throat, Kate slammed the apartment door behind her and stepped out into the night.

The flight passed in a blur of turbulence and fitful dozing, Kate's mind too consumed with worst-case scenarios to allow for true rest. By the time the plane touched down at O'Hare, she was jittery with nerves and stale coffee, her eyes gritty and bloodshot.

She shouldered her way off the plane and through the terminal, bypassing baggage claim and silently thanking past Kate for having the foresight to pack light. The sky outside the floor-to-ceiling windows was just beginning to lighten, the first pale fingers of dawn streaking the horizon as she boarded the complimentary shuttle that took her to the car rental plaza.

The attendant at the car rental pickup desk was far too chipper this early in the morning, her megawatt smile grating against Kate's frayed nerves. She scrawled her signature on the agreement, snatched the key fob from the counter, and wove through the rows of identical sedans in the cool and silent parking garage until she located her assigned vehicle.

Tossing her bag into the backseat, Kate slid behind the wheel and closed her eyes, resting her forehead against the cool leather steering wheel. She allowed herself a single moment to just breathe, to try and center herself before the coming ordeal.

The car purred to life beneath her, and she navigated the labyrinth parking structure on autopilot, finally merging onto the highway. She merged into the sparse early morning traffic, the radio dial tuned to a classic rock station, the same one Walter always listened to in the car, in the garage, in the house. It carried her back to a time when the house resonated with the raw power of Creedence Clearwater Revival, the heartfelt ballads of Bob Seger, the intricate musicianship of Rush, the electrifying riffs of Led Zeppelin, the bluesy rock of Foghat, the psychedelic soundscapes of Pink Floyd, the explosive energy of The Who, or the soaring harmonies of Boston. These were the anthems of her father, the soundtrack to his life.

As the opening chords of Springsteen's "Tramps Like Us" filled the sedan, the Boss's voice softened slightly at the bridge, tinged with a touch of vulnerability as he sang about the yearning for connection and belonging. Kate was catapulted back in time, memories of her father flooding in with each familiar riff and lyric. She saw herself sprawled out on the plush rust-colored carpet of her dad's study playing *Ape Escape: On the Loose* on the PSP he'd got for her ninth birthday. Walter engulfed in his worn chocolate BarcaLounger, its familiar creak each time he settled into it, his foot tapping along to the rhythm of whatever song played on the stereo. Walter sitting at the dining room table meticulously constructing a model airplane. Walter dressed in greasy overalls, the clang of tools ringing out as he leaned into the engine well of his 1970 Ford F-100 pickup. Walter, quietly focused while he crafted delicate fishing flies under the warm glow of his study lamp.

But most of all, she saw the way he'd looked at her mother —like she was the sunrise and the sunset, the axis around which his world spun. Saw the light in his eyes slowly dim in the months following Eleanor's death, a little more of him slipping away each day.

Grief rose in her throat, hot and choking. Kate tightened her fingers on the steering wheel until her knuckles ached, blinking back the tears that blurred the road ahead. She couldn't fall apart, not now. Not when her father needed her to be strong the way he'd always been for her, the stalwart oak standing tall amid the fiercest storms.

But even as she squared her jaw and swallowed past the ache in her chest, Kate couldn't quite shake the sense of dread curling in her stomach like a cold fist. Because whatever waited for her at Walter's bedside, whatever condition she found him in...she knew, with a bone-deep certainty, that their lives would never be the same.

That the simple, golden days of her childhood were gone, lost to the mists of time and memory. That the man who'd been her port in every tempest, her unshakable constant in a chaotic world, might soon be ripped away, leaving her anchorless and adrift.

Jaw clenched against the sob building in her throat, Kate pressed down on the accelerator, propelling the car forward as if she could outrun the fear nipping at her heels. The highway unfurled before her, carrying her inexorably toward a future she wasn't ready to face.

But ready or not, it was time to be the daughter Walter needed. To wade into the darkness and find a way to guide them both back to the light. No matter how deep the shadows grew, or how tightly they threatened to pull her under.

Nightmares and Warnings

Kate leaned back into the uncomfortable chair, the rough blue fabric scratchy against her warm skin and smelling faintly of industrial cleaner. The

ER waiting room was a study in hushed tones, the only other occupant a middle-aged Latina woman counting rosary beads as they slipped silently through her calloused, arthritic fingers.

The hypnotic hum of the overhead lights was broken only by the occasional swish of the automatic doors connecting the patient floor to the nurses' station. Kate's heavy lids pulled her eyes closed and soon she drifted off into a restless doze.

Some time later, she stirred awake, slumped awkwardly in the chair. The Latina woman was gone and bright sunlight now spilled through the entrance doors. The plump redheaded nurse at the reception desk noticed Kate's movement and walked over.

"Ms. Emerson?" Her voice was soft but startled Kate fully awake.

"Yes," Kate mumbled, forcing herself upright. Unease prickled the back of her neck.

"I'm Nurse Kim. You spoke to Melissa earlier." The nurse's smile faltered slightly as she settled into the adjacent chair. "Sorry for the wait. It's a bit hectic back there." She nodded toward the unseen chaos of the patient floor.

Kate managed a tight smile, her voice cracking. "Is there any news on my father?"

Nurse Kim pursed her lips. "Not yet, honey. Dr. Phillips will be done with rounds shortly and may have an update for you then."

A cold dread settled in Kate's stomach as the room seemed to close in. "Can you tell me anything about what happened?"

"We're not entirely sure yet," Nurse Kim said gently. "The police received a call from a neighbor who heard noises from your father's house. They found Walter unconscious and the paramedics brought him in around 1 AM. He was unresponsive."

Feeling numb, Kate asked, "Can I see him?"

"Of course, but not until later once they get him settled in a room. One of us will call you then." Nurse Kim's voice was soft with sympathy.

Approaching footsteps made them both look up as a tall man in a white coat stopped beside them. "Ms. Emerson? I'm Dr. Phillips, so sorry for your worry."

"Do you know what happened to my father?" Kate asked, her throat tight.

Dr. Phillips sighed. "It appears he's had a massive stroke. We need to run more tests to assess the extent of the damage. Unfortunately, I can't give you anything conclusive at this point. We'll monitor him closely today and keep him comfortable."

Knuckles white as she gripped the chair arms, Kate pleaded, "Can I please see him?"

"Not just yet, but as soon as we get him in a room, which may take a few hours." Dr Phillips paused. "In the meantime, Ms. Emerson, you should go home and rest. This will be a difficult journey. We can connect you with a psychologist if you'd like to talk to someone."

Kate shook her head, the edges of her vision blurring. "No, thank you."

Minutes later, she left the waiting room in a daze, walking on autopilot to locate her rental car in the parking garage across the street. Settling heavily into the driver's seat, Kate took a deep breath, trying to calm her frayed nerves.

Her last conversation with Walter several months ago replayed in her mind. He'd seemed fine then, hadn't mentioned any health concerns. In fact, he appeared to be coping much better with her mother's death, even seeing a grief counselor, taking up painting as therapy. Everything had seemed well. Of course, Walter wouldn't tell her how he was feeling, like a typical man. He always kept his emotions bottled up, preferring to suffer in silence than to burden her with his worries.

Exhausted and emotionally spent, Kate just wanted to get to her father's house and rest for a while. But when she pushed the ignition button, the car refused to start. She shifted her foot on the brake pedal but the car remained stubbornly silent.

"Piece of shit!" Her palms slammed against the steering wheel in frustration. Leaning forward to rest her forehead on the cool leather, she squeezed her eyes shut, jaw clenched. "Just fucking great."

With a frustrated sigh, she reached under the dash, fumbling for the hood latch. A sharp click echoed as it released, and she pushed open the driver's door and got out. She slammed the door shut, her footsteps echoing through the parking garage as she made her way to the front of the car.

Her fingers traced the underside of the hood, finding the small lip and lifting it upward. The hood rose with a creak, revealing a confusing jumble of engine components. Gleaming metal parts intertwined with a chaotic web of wires, their multicolored insulation barely visible beneath layers of dust and grime. Thick rubber hoses snaked through the cramped space, their purpose a mystery to her untrained eye. It was a scene of organized chaos, a symphony of engineering she couldn't begin to decipher.

As she straightened up, ready to close the hood, a flicker of movement in her peripheral vision made Kate start. There on the Toyota's roof perched a single crow, its oily black feathers gleaming under the bright lamps. The bird's uncanny, intelligent gaze pierced through her as it cocked its head.

Then, with an unnatural, almost human-like caw, the crow spoke a single word that hung in the air and echoed through the garage: "*Close.*"

Kate stepped back, heart pounding.

Crows didn't talk, but she was certain she'd heard it clearly.

Feigning toward the bird, she flapped her hands. "Shoo!"

The crow responded with a few aggressive steps forward,

flapping its wings. *"Close,"* it repeated before launching into flight directly at her face.

Yelping, Kate instinctively ducked and raised her hands, but at the last second, the crow veered left and disappeared into the upper levels of the garage. Still crouched, she looked over her shoulder, half expecting it to return and attack with its sharp beak. But thirty tense seconds passed without incident.

Rising on shaky legs, Kate retrieved her purse and weekender bag from the car, along with the roadside assistance card from the glovebox. Too tired and stressed to deal with the rental issue now, she decided to walk the eighteen blocks to her father's place and handle the car later after getting some much-needed rest.

Forty minutes later, standing on the porch of her childhood home, Kate dug through her purse for the front door key she'd last used two years ago when she returned home for her mother's funeral. A wave of that same sorrow washed over her now, mingling with the worry and fear over Walter's condition.

But the thin stitching of the interior pocket where she'd tucked it away had worn through, allowing the key to slip into the purse's lining. It was as if the purse itself had conspired to keep the key hidden from her.

"Fuck my life," she muttered, exasperated. Setting her bags down with a thud that echoed the frustration in her voice, she knelt and stretched her finger as far as it would go into the small hole, the cold metal biting into her skin. Sweat beaded on her brow as she desperately tried to grasp the key, her nails scraping against the smooth surface. But it remained frustratingly out of reach, taunting her with its jingle each time she moved.

A pulsing anger throbbed in Kate's temples, painting her cheeks with a fiery blush. All she craved was a moment of respite within the cool haven of her home, yet this obstinate key defied her. Gritting her teeth, she jammed a finger from her free hand into the stubborn seam, adding to the pressure. With a strained grunt, she tore the stubborn lining apart, creating a gaping three-inch tear.

Triumphantly, she plunged her hand inside and reclaimed the elusive key, a surge of relief flooding through her. Ignoring her bags on the porch for now, Kate strode purposefully to the door, the key clicking into the deadbolt with a satisfying thunk. Pushing the heavy door inward, she nudged the screen door aside with her foot, grabbing her purse and bag and stepped inside.

Closing the door behind her, she was met with a pungent aroma that instantly made her nose wrinkle. It was a peculiar scent, a strange concoction of vanilla sweetness undercut by the acrid remnants of stale cigarette smoke. The sight that greeted her was no less jarring. The living room was a scene of utter chaos, a jumble of discarded takeout containers, clothes tossed haphazardly, and overflowing ashtrays scattered on every available surface. In the kitchen, the sink had become a repository for days' worth of unwashed dishes, while the overflowing garbage can strained to contain its bulging, overfilled bag.

"Jesus, Dad, what's happened to you?" Kate whispered, her voice barely audible as she took in the disarray of the living room. This level of mess was totally unlike the orderly, organized father she remembered. Clearly, he had lost all motivation and was just going through the motions of existing.

A pang of guilt washed over her as she realized how oblivious she had been to his true mental state. Blinded by the allure of her bustling life in Los Angeles, she had failed to truly see him, to recognize the quiet desperation lurking beneath his usual stoicism. He had always been a man of few words, preferring to bear his burdens in silence.

Exhausted but unable to ignore the squalor, Kate spent the next hour attacking the most visible signs of neglect. She tossed expired food, scrubbed sticky dishes, and corralled the worst of the clutter into overflowing trash bags. The kitchen remained a disaster zone, with grime clinging to every surface and a suspicious film coating the floor, but it was a start. A wave of fatigue washed over her, and she knew she couldn't tackle the rest tonight. The thought of disinfecting the counters or mopping the floor filled her with dread. She would rest for now, and face the rest of the mess another day.

By late afternoon, her stomach growled with a familiar hunger, reminding her that she hadn't eaten a single bite all day. With no car at her disposal—she was far too tired to go out anyway—she ordered Chinese delivery from a favorite local spot. She made a nest on the sofa where she lounged until the food arrived. The aroma of General Tso's chicken made her mouth instantly water. She settled onto the floor in front of the coffee table, her makeshift dining spot, and switched on the television. The drone of the local news provided a low hum of background noise as she savored each bite.

Around seven, Kate could barely keep her eyes open any longer. With a sigh, she scraped the remnants of her dinner into a plastic container and stowed it in the refrigerator. She washed the lone fork and plate she had used and dried her hands on a dish towel. Switching off the television, she trudged up the stairs to the second floor to her old bedroom. She discovered Walter had turned it into an art studio.

Walter mentioned taking up painting as a form of grief therapy recommended by the grief counselor, but she hadn't realized the extent of his dedication. He had easels and canvases, paints, brushes, palettes, and mason jars of clear fluids she assumed were solvents for cleaning brushes.

What she discovered was not a casual hobby, but a full-fledged artist's studio. Multiple easels held canvases in various stages of completion. An organized chaos of paint tubes, brushes of varying sizes, and well-used palettes occupied a large work table. Several mason jars filled with clear liquids—likely solvents or mediums.

The room was in a disarray. The chair in front of the desk

now lay overturned, its legs pointing toward the ceiling like skeletal limbs. Scattered across the floor, amid the paint cans, brushes, and other art supplies, were torn pages from a sketchbook, their ink-stained edges. Beside the door, an easel lay on its side, the canvas that had sat upon it was on the floor, face down.

Righting the easel, Kate picked up the fallen canvas. It was heavier than she expected, solid and sturdy in its wooden frame. The unfinished painting was a scene from a local park, a large oak tree at the center of the canvas, its branches reaching toward the sky like outstretched arms. Standing beside the tree was a woman in a light pink sweater and faded blue jeans. Her hair, a rich auburn, was pulled back in a loose ponytail, and her posture suggested a quiet contentment. Though her father hadn't yet painted in the details of the face, Kate was sure the woman was her mother, Eleanor. The resemblance was uncanny, not just in the physical features, but in the essence of the woman portrayed. The skill far exceeded her expectations for a beginning painter. Walter clearly had a knack for capturing not just the likeness of his subjects, but their spirit as well.

Setting the unfinished portrait back on the easel, Kate turned to organize the rest of the disheveled studio. She picked up the overturned chair and scattered art supplies, methodically placing them on the folding table. But as she bent to retrieve a fallen paintbrush, she froze. In the dim light filtering through the dusty window, she spotted a wooden

Ouija board lying on the floor. A chill ran down her spine as she stared at the unexpected object, its presence an unsettling mystery in the otherwise familiar space.

"What on earth?" she murmured, a sense of bewilderment washing over her. Walter, of all people, the pragmatic skeptic, the man who scoffed at anything remotely mystical or spiritual, was the last person she'd ever associate with such an object. She found herself momentarily frozen, staring at the ornately carved board resting on his desk.

A Ouija board. Her mind raced, trying to reconcile the incongruity. *Did he intend to incorporate it into one of his paintings*? Curiosity piqued, she reached out and gently lifted the board, its smooth surface cool beneath her fingertips.

It was heavier than expected, not the flimsy cardboard she had anticipated, but rather a solid, half-inch thick plank of wood. The wood was stained a deep, mahogany brown, hinting at a craftsmanship that went beyond mere novelty. A coat of lacquer gave it a slick, glossy feel, the smooth surface cool to the touch.

She placed the board on the desk, the soft thud echoing in the otherwise silent room. The planchette, a heart-shaped piece of wood with a small magnifying window in the center lay upside down, its three felt-tipped feet pointing upward, like three curious eyes staring up at her.

An odd curiosity stirred within her as she examined the elaborate Ouija board set, her fingers tracing the intricate engravings and glossy finish. The board and planchette appeared to be handmade, not something purchased from a mass-market retailer. The smooth, cool surface of the board felt like polished mahogany, each letter and number meticulously etched into its depths. The planchette, a crescent moon carved from pearlescent shell, rested lightly in her palm, its polished surface cool against her skin. Each detail spoke of meticulous craftsmanship, of hours spent pouring over the design and execution of this singular object. A tingle of anticipation prickled at the base of her neck, a quiet hum of energy that seemed to emanate from the board itself.

She turned the planchette over in her hand, her fingers tracing the cool, smooth surface of the wooden heart. The moonlight filtering through the window glinted off the glass lens, casting a spectral glow on her face. Impulsively, she raised the planchette to her eye and peered through the round window, her gaze drawn to the floor where the painting had rested only moments ago.

Kate gasped, her breath catching in her throat. Through the planchette's window, the hardwood floor beneath where the canvas had lain appeared blackened and blistered in a large, irregular shape, as if charred by incredible heat. She quickly lowered her hand, the planchette's weight suddenly heavy in her palm.

The flooring was unblemished.

The room felt colder now, the shadows deeper. Had she imagined the mark on the floor?

A prickle of adrenaline flooded through her veins as she

tentatively lifted the planchette once more. The eerie burn mark materialized again. Her gaze through the planchette drifted upward to the painting and a gasp escaped her lips. The portrait remained unchanged except for one terrifying detail: the woman's previously blank face was now twisted into an expression of unmitigated horror, eyes widened and mouth agape in a silent scream. The most unsettling detail, however, was the figure that loomed over the woman's cowering form. A gaunt, spectral silhouette, its elongated fingers digging into her shoulder, seemed to drain the very life from the portrait. It was a scene that defied logic, a macabre tableau etched across the canvas.

The abrupt thud of Kate's body hitting the desk sent a tremor through the planchette, which she hastily lowered with shaking hands. A wave of nausea washed over her as she tried to process the scene she had just witnessed. This couldn't be possible. Her gaze snapped back to the painting, but all she saw was the unfinished portrait, its canvas devoid of the shadowy figure that had momentarily appeared. The scorch mark on the floor, too, was gone. With a dry swallow, Kate raised the planchette once more, her fingers tightening around its smooth edges. It quivered slightly as she focused her vision through the central opening, her breath held in anticipation.

The painting was unchanged. The featureless woman was as she'd been. Panning downward, the charred floor was unmarked.

Gently placing the planchette back on the desk, Kate exhaled a shaky breath she hadn't realized she'd been holding. The scene she had just witnessed defied explanation, leaving her momentarily rooted in disbelief. Moving as if in a trance, she knelt on the floor, running her fingers across the spot where she'd seen the distinct burn mark. The smooth surface of the hardwood, coated in a protective wax seal, offered no evidence of the strange phenomenon.

Rising from her knees, she examined the canvas, searching for the subtlest change in brushstroke or color. At this distance, she observed the careful brush strokes and fine details of her father's hand upon the canvas. She gently ran the ball of her thumb over the faceless woman and felt the slight texture of the dried acrylic paint. A sense of unease settled upon her, the silence of the room growing heavy with unanswered questions.

"I'm losing it," she whispered, her voice barely audible over the rhythmic thumping of her own heartbeat. The words echoed in the hollow silence of the room. Clearly her mind was playing tricks after the overwhelming events and sleepless hours of this nightmarish day.

With a sigh that carried a hint of wistfulness, Kate switched off the studio light, casting the room in a gentle darkness. The soft click of the door echoed her weariness. Sleeping in her parent's bedroom wasn't going to happen. She grabbed a pillow and blanket from the hall closet and made up a bed on the living room couch. Within minutes of switching off the lamp, she fell into a deep slumber.

Within the dream's murky depths, Kate materialized inside Walter's studio, her horrified gaze locked on the twisted portrait. Her mother's terrified face, twisted into a mask of terror, her eyes wide with fright, stared back at her from the canvas. Beside her mother's image in the painting, a nightmarish figure emerged from the shadows, its long, gnarled fingers digging into her mother's shoulder. The creature's form was barely discernible, a vague silhouette against the painted backdrop. Its ember-red eyes rose to meet her own, glowing like hot coals in the inky darkness of its face.

A hand suddenly clamped down upon Kate's shoulder, biting into her flesh through the thin fabric of her shirt. She screamed and whirled around, her eyes wide with alarm. Relief washed over her when she found Walter standing there.

"Dad!" She flung her arms around him, shaking.

Walter's fingers dug into Katie's upper arms, his grip firm but not painful as he held her back. He lowered his head until their gazes met, his brow furrowed with an intensity that stole her breath. The usual warmth in his eyes had been replaced by a chilling resolve. "Katie," he said, his voice low and urgent, "you need to shut the door. Now. Do you understand?" The words hung heavy in the air between them, each syllable a stark reminder of the unseen danger lurking just beyond the threshold.

"What door? Dad, you're not making sense!" Kate's voice

rose an octave, her confusion giving way to a prickle of unease.

"Close it before it's too late!" Walter's voice was a harsh rasp, his fingers digging into Kate's arms with a bruising intensity. "It cannot be allowed to come through!"

"I don't understand! What are you—"

Her words died in her throat, a strangled gasp escaping her lips as an unseen force wrenched Walter from her side, hurtling him backward through the window and into the darkness beyond. For a split second, Kate stood frozen, the echo of shattering glass ringing in her ears. Then, adrenaline surged through her veins, snapping her out of her paralysis. She whirled around, her heart pounding in her chest as she stumbled toward the door, desperate to escape the unseen terror that had invaded the room—

—and found herself face to face with the shadow being, its nightmarish visage mere inches from her own as it leaned over her, impossibly tall. The creature's form seemed to waver and distort, an amorphous silhouette that defied definition. Suffocating heat rolled off its oily skin, each pore shimmering with a sickly luminescence. A fetid stench, like rotting flesh mixed with sulfur, filled her nostrils, triggering a wave of nausea that threatened to overwhelm her. Kate's throat constricted as she tried to scream, but no sound emerged. Her lungs burned, desperate for air, but the suffocating presence of the creature seemed to have stolen her breath. All she could do was stare into its burning scarlet eyes, twin orbs of malevolence that seemed to sear into her very soul, probing the depths of her fears and feeding on her terror.

On the sofa, Kate thrashed in her sleep. Fear radiated through her body like a flash fire before the nightmare suddenly slipped into another dream, and her stream of consciousness shifted, plunging her into a new realm of twilight images. The once terrifying visions dissipated, replaced by a kaleidoscope of fragmented scenes that flickered and danced behind her closed eyelids. Her breathing gradually slowed, the tension in her muscles uncoiling as the dream's ephemeral threads wove a new tapestry in her mind.

Unbeknownst to Kate, up in the studio, with a soft sound like a zipper, a six inch gash suddenly split the unfinished painting down the center, cleaving the shadowy figure and featureless woman in two as if sliced by an unseen blade. The rift gaped open like a festering wound.

Ominous change was coming. The door between worlds had cracked ajar. And something hateful and hungry lurked at the threshold, eager to slip through and wreak its malice on the unsuspecting.

Only Kate stood in its way, though she didn't know it yet. For now, she continued to dream. But the true nightmare was only just beginning.

A TWIST OF FATE

Kate woke to sunlight knifing through the living room blinds, casting a zebra pattern of light and shadow on the walls. A low groan escaped her as she threw an arm over her eyes to block out the intrusive brightness, lingering in the hazy space between sleep and wakefulness for a few precious minutes.

The twisted bedding slid to the floor as she stretched, muscles groaning in complaint. Her spine released a series of satisfying cracks as she arched her back. A dull throb pulsed behind her temples and her neck ached, a reminder of the fitful sleep she'd managed on the lumpy sofa. With a sigh, she leaned forward, elbows digging into her knees as she snatched up her phone from the coffee table.

10:03 AM glowed on the screen of her iPhone in large white numerals. There had been no updates from the hospital about Walter's condition, and with each passing minute, the silence amplified her anxiety. The longer the silence stretched, the more her worry metastasized.

Dragging herself to the bathroom, her heavy footsteps echoed loudly in the too-quiet house. She cranked the shower handles and stripped mechanically, leaving yesterday's clothes puddled on the tiles. As steam filled the small space, she confronted her reflection while brushing her teeth.

Her chestnut hair was flattened on one side and wildly mussed on the other. The faint imprint of a sofa cushion seam lined her left cheek. Exhausted green eyes stared back at her from a face pale with strain.

"You look like shit," she told her haggard mirror-self bluntly.

Under the spray of near-scalding water, Kate felt the knots

in her shoulders begin to unwind. The steady rhythm of water drumming on her skull and the white noise hum of the vent fan created a cocoon of temporary peace, easing the persistent ache in her head and loosening the tightness in her neck.

She lingered under the warm spray until the water began to cool. Reluctantly, she stepped out of the shower and reached for a towel, drying off quickly. Spying her dirty clothes on the floor, she remembered with a frustrated sigh that her overnight bag was still downstairs. Muttering under her breath, she wrapped herself in the damp terry cloth and padded out into the upstairs hallway, shivering as the cool air hit her damp skin.

Kate paused outside Walter's closed studio door, the unanswered questions from last night swarming in her head like angry flies. The memory of that damn Ouija board—an object so at odds with her rational, level-headed father—left her unsettled. What possible reason could he have for owning such a thing, let alone using it?

Did he use it? How could he manage the board alone? You needed at least two people, right?

Kate's stomach twisted with a familiar unease, a cold tendril of dread uncoiling within her. She knew her father, his unwavering pragmatism, the stanch rationality that had defined his entire existence. The idea of Walter dabbling in the occult, the shadowy realms of superstition and blind spiritualism, was a stark departure from everything she knew. The notion of such profound meaninglessness threatened to upend her understanding of the world, leaving her adrift in a sea of uncertainty.

What the actual fuck had transpired in the studio that left it looking like a crime scene? Had Walter collapsed there mid-stroke, flailing and writhing across the room until unconsciousness claimed him?

On the other side of the door, she pictured Walter, lost in the creation of beauty, his brush sweeping across the canvas. Then, without warning, his breath hitched, each inhale a desperate gasp. Sweat beaded on his brow, his face paling. The world around him seemed to distort, his vision tunneling. Her father's once sharp mind was now a captive in a failing body. His gaze darted around the room, unfocused, searching for an escape from this nightmare. His face, those warm paternal features she knew so well, contorted with terror. His strong, steady form twisted and contorted, stumbling across the room, knocking over the chair, bumping the table, sending art supplies scattering. He flailed, losing balance, crashing into the easel, collapsing with the canvas. As he lay there, strength draining from his limbs, she could feel his desperate desire to communicate, to make someone understand the silent scream trapped within. Then, as darkness finally claimed him, his eyes fluttered shut, his body falling still.

Kate shook her head, pushing the images away. There was no use dwelling on what happened to Walter behind that door. The past was the past, and she needed to focus on the present, on getting an update on his condition.

Downstairs, Kate yanked on clean jeans and a t-shirt, then perched on the edge of the couch. She worked her fingers through the tangles in her damp hair as she dialed the hospital. The shift nurse that answered sounded brusque and hurried.

"We have a room assigned for Walter, but he hasn't been transferred yet," the nurse informed her, her voice a preoccupied monotone. "Likely this afternoon, around 3 or 4. We'll call you as soon as he's settled and able to have visitors."

Kate's grip tightened on the phone, her knuckles turning white. "Can't you give me any more information?" she asked, her voice sharp with worry. "What's his current condition?" Each word was a struggle, her usual composure cracking under the pressure.

"I'm sorry, but you'll need to discuss specifics with the doctor."

"Is he available *now*?" Kate winced inwardly at the sharpness in her voice, but the urgency of her situation had eclipsed any semblance of social grace.

"I'm afraid he's making rounds at the moment."

Kate hissed out a breath, the sound sharp and ragged, as she fought back the urge to lash out at the nurse. The woman was merely following protocol, but the impersonal efficiency of it all grated against Kate's raw nerves. "All right," she managed, the word a dry, bitter taste in her mouth. "Thank you."

Ending the call, she immediately punched in the number

for her office, the force of her finger betraying the tension simmering beneath her calm facade. Cindy, her unflappable assistant, answered on the first ring, her steady voice momentarily eased Kate's anxieties. Assured that everything was under control, Kate felt a sliver of tension release its grip on her.

"Just focus on your dad right now. We've got things handled here, don't worry about us."

"Thanks, Cindy. If anything comes up, anything at all, call me." Kate disconnected.

Restless energy buzzed throughout her body. Her stomach growled demandingly. Groceries were what she needed. Something mundane and normal to occupy her time and divert her mind from the quagmire of what-ifs. Anything was better than sitting here drowning in uncertainty.

Shrugging on her jacket, she found the rental car company's roadside assistance card in her purse and dialed the number. The agent apologized profusely for the Camry's breakdown and assured her they would collect it from the hospital garage. However, a replacement wouldn't be available until the next day, adding another minor frustration to an already difficult morning.

With a heavy sigh, Kate summoned a Lyft, her mind a whirlwind of worry as the driver navigated to the nearest supermarket. Wandering the fluorescent-lit aisles, she mechanically dropped items into her basket, her thoughts constantly returning to Walter wondering what had happened to him in that damn studio—she was sure that was where he'd had his stroke—and wondered if he would recover.

Possibilities twisted and mutated in her mind, a merry-go-round of dread. She was so lost in the labyrinth of worst-case scenarios that she nearly slammed into another shopper's cart, jerking her back to reality with a start.

"Katie Emerson?"

That voice, warm and achingly familiar even after all these years, caught her off guard. Her head snapped up and there amid the chilly mist of the refrigerated section, stood James Nowak.

Time had left its mark on him, carving shallow lines into the face. A jagged scar slashed across his left cheek, a visible reminder of his military service. His eyes though…those remained unchanged. Pale brown, warm and familiar, they held a hint of mischief, inviting her to share a lighthearted moment.

"Jimmy Nowak." Saying his name aloud after so long felt surreal, the syllables clumsy and foreign in her mouth.

"My God, Katie…it's been forever." He stepped closer, arms coming up for an awkward hug. The brief contact zinged through her like an electrical current, the years falling away for that suspended moment.

"Six years," she confirmed as they stepped back, the weight of that time settling between them once more. Her gaze lingered briefly on the scar. "You look good. Changed, but good."

Color crept up James's neck, warming his face. He reached up to touch the scar self-consciously. "That's what a stint in the Army will do to you," he deflected with a rueful chuckle.

"So I've heard. But you're back."

He shifted his weight, clearing his throat. "Yeah, a little over a year now." Silence stretched, threaded with tension. "So, uh...what brings you back to the Windy City? Not that grocery shopping isn't riveting, but last I heard you were tearing up the legal scene in LA."

The casual mention of her life on the west coast brought the full weight of reality crashing back down on her, a somber reminder of why she was here, now, in this grocery store. Kate swallowed thickly against the sudden lump in her throat, her fingers tightening reflexively around the handles of the shopping basket as if anchoring herself to the present moment.

"It's my dad," she began, her voice trembling slightly, the words catching in her throat. "He's...not well." A wave of sadness washed over her face, making the strain of the past few days evident. James's eyes softened with empathy, noticing the exhaustion etched into her features, the tightness around her mouth betraying the brave front she put up. He could see past the forced smile, recognizing the deep worry she carried for her father.

"Shit, I'm so sorry. What happened?" His brow furrowed with worry, and he instinctively leaned in, his eyes searching your face for answers.

Kate took a deep, shaky breath, steadying herself against

THE DEVIL'S DOORWAY

the wave of emotions threatening to engulf her. She fixed her gaze on the meticulously arranged rows of frozen goods behind the man, finding solace in their predictable order.

"I received a late-night call last night," she began, her voice barely a whisper. "A neighbor heard a disturbance at the house, and when the police arrived, they found my dad unresponsive. I caught the first flight out here this morning, but the doctors but the doctors can't or won't tell me anything useful yet. I haven't even been allowed to see him." The words felt like a physical blow, a knot of grief and anger tightening in her chest.

James's fingers twitched involuntarily at his side, a familiar impulse to reach out and offer comfort surging within him. He hesitated, knowing it wasn't his place anymore. Time and distance had eroded the closeness they once shared, leaving behind a chasm he wasn't sure how to bridge. Yet, a persistent voice in the back of his mind whispered that he still cared deeply, that a part of him had never stopped wondering what could have been, had their paths diverged differently.

With deliberate gentleness, he placed his hand over hers on the basket handle. t was a small gesture, unspoken yet filled with a silent understanding and comfort. Her gaze lifted to meet his, and in the depths of her storm-tossed green eyes, a shimmering film of unshed tears revealed the depth of her sorrow. For the briefest of moments, a raw vulnerability flickered across her features, a raw ache of loss before she quickly masked it with composure.

"Walter's one tough son of a bitch," James remarked, a hint of admiration and nostalgia in his voice. "Back in high school, I remember him striking absolute terror into the hearts of any guy who even dared to so much as glance in your direction. Your old man was a force to be reckoned with."

A hint of amusement touched his lips as a smile briefly flitted across his face. "I didn't know you two kept in touch."

James shrugged, a hint of bashfulness coloring his cheeks. "He stops by my bookshop every now and then, usually for a cup of coffee and a chat. He's quite the aficionado when it comes to WWII history, you know."

Kate's eyes widened in surprise, a spark of curiosity momentarily brightening her face and pushing aside the veil of sadness that had settled over her. "You have your own shop?" she inquired, her voice a mix of wonder and intrigue.

A flush crept up his cheeks as he ducked his head, a shy smile playing on his lips. "Yeah," he admitted, a hint of amusement sparkling in his eyes, "it's a small bookstore and coffee shop called The Caffeinated Page." The name brought a playful grin to his face, as if inviting her to share in the clever wordplay.

"That's wonderful, Jimmy. I'm truly thrilled for you." Her sincerity was clear in her voice.

"Maybe, if you have time while you're here...you could swing by sometime? Let me caffeinate you and bore you with small-talk?" His tone was deliberately nonchalant, but a hint of nervousness peeked through his words.

Kate paused, a flicker of their shared history passing between them. "That would be nice," she agreed, choosing her words carefully. "Once I have a better understanding of my dad's situation and outlook, I'll try to make some time."

A shadow of disappointment crossed James's face, but he quickly recovered, offering a genuine smile. "No problem at all. I understand completely. You've got a lot on your plate right now." He took a step back, creating a respectful distance between them.

An unspoken understanding lingered in the air, a shared moment of connection. Kate, finally breaking the comfortable silence, gestured with her half-filled basket. "I probably should finish up my shopping and get back home," she said with a gentle smile, "Just in case the hospital calls with any updates."

"Of course, you're absolutely right," James responded, a hint of reluctance in his voice. "I didn't mean to hold you up." But the truth was, if given the chance, he would have happily spent the rest of the day chatting with Kate right there in the middle of the aisle, their carts abandoned in favor of rekindling their friendship.

"It was good to see you, Jimmy. Really." She attempted a smile but it fell a few watts short of convincing. He returned it anyway.

"You too, Katie. I'm here if you need anything, okay? Even just to talk."

She nodded silently, her throat tight with unspoken words, and quickly made her way down the aisle, the sting of unshed tears blurring her vision. James watched her retreating figure, a profound sadness settling heavily within him.

Fate, it seemed, had a twisted sense of humor. Throwing Katie back into his orbit after six years, but under the worst circumstances. A part of him, the part that would always be the reckless boy who loved her, wanted to chase after her. Wrap her in his arms and never let go.

But he wasn't that boy anymore and she wasn't the same girl. Life and time had battered and changed them both, shaping them into strangers masquerading in familiar skin. Still, he couldn't quell the stubborn spark of hope flaring to life in his chest.

Hope that, even amid the painful circumstances of their reunion, they might find their way back to each other. That they could resurrect the easy camaraderie, the intimate connection, that time and distance had strained but never quite severed.

He would give her space, let her focus on Walter. But when the dust settled, when she had room to breathe again...he'd be waiting. Coffee and conversation, a chance to rediscover who they were now, to each other and to themselves. It was more than he'd dared to dream of for the past six years.

Toting his own groceries to the checkout, James let himself imagine it. Katie perched on the counter at his shop, hands wrapped around a steaming mug, green eyes sparkling at him over the rim as she laughed at some stupid joke. It was a pretty thought, fragile as spun glass. But he'd cradle it carefully, nurturing it until it had a chance to become reality.

Outside the store, as Kate waited for her ride, emotionally and physically wrung out, the slap of footsteps on pavement made her turn. James loped toward her, waving.

"Still here?" His eyes wrinkled at the corners when he smiled.

She blinked at him. "I'm waiting for my Lyft."

A warmth spread through him. Perhaps fate wasn't done with them yet. "Cancel it. I'll drive you home."

"My dad's place is out of your way."

He shrugged, adjusting the grip on his shopping bags. "Not really. It's on the way to the shop."

Kate hesitated, a mix of exhaustion and a yearning for familiar comfort tugging at her. "I don't want to impose..."

"You're not." His voice was firm, laced with affection and exasperation. "C'mon, Emerson. Let me give you a lift. For old times' sake."

Something in his gaze, open and earnest, made her resistance crumble. "Okay. Thanks." She offered a wan smile and followed him to his car, canceling the Lyft with a few quick taps on her phone.

They rode in silence for a bit, the unspoken words

lingering between them. Finally James cracked a window, letting in a gust of fresh air and, along with it, a surge of courage.

"Why didn't you use Walter's truck?" He glanced at her briefly, his curiosity piqued.

A huff, almost a laugh. "The Ford? Not a chance. You know how Dad guards that thing with his life." In her best imitation of Walter, she said, "That car is a museum piece, Katie-bird, not something you take out for a Sunday drive."

He chuckled, genuinely impressed by her uncanny ability to mimic her father's mannerisms and speech patterns. "What about renting a car to get you around while you're here?"

Her sigh was heavy, laden with exhaustion. "My rental decided to give up the ghost," she said, a weary edge creeping into her voice. "Died right there in the hospital parking garage last night. And of course, they can't get a replacement here until tomorrow. Maybe. Honestly, it feels like the universe is conspiring against me lately."

"That blows." Empathy softened his voice. "Look, if you ever find yourself stranded again, don't hesitate to call me." It was a peace offering disguised as a casual suggestion.

"My own personal Uber, huh?" The echo of their old banter returned, a familiar melody slightly off-key, yet still as effortless as drawing breath.

"Something like that." He pulled up outside her father's house and killed the engine. An expectant hush fell, the air heavy with potential.

Kate gnawed her bottom lip, fingers plucking at a loose thread on her jeans. "I'd invite you in but..."

"No, it's fine. You've got a lot on your plate," he reassured her, his voice softer than intended. He popped the trunk and retrieved her grocery bags, something fierce and protective stirring in his chest at how small she looked weighted down with them.

"Thanks, Jimmy," she said, her voice thick with emotion. Gratitude was there, certainly, but something else lingered beneath the surface. A vulnerability, a depth of feeling that colored the simple words. "For everything."

Clearing the sudden thickness from his throat, James dug in his back pocket and extracted a slightly dog-eared business card. He pressed it into her palm, fingers lingering a breath too long.

"I meant what I said before. Anything you need, even if it's just to talk...call me. Please." His eyes bored into hers, hoping she would accept his offer of support.

Her fingers curled around the card, a small comfort against the overwhelming fear and loneliness. "I will. Promise."

He stepped back, letting her walk away. At the door, she turned back and their eyes met. A complex mixture of longing and hope played across his face. She raised a hand in farewell and then slipped inside, the solid click of the latch echoing like a gunshot in the hushed afternoon.

James stood rooted a moment longer, staring at the weathered door. The urge to march up and knock, to offer to stay and help, to hold her until the world righted itself, was a living ache in his bones.

She'll call, he told himself as he drove away. She'd let him be there for her, in whatever way she'd allow. He just had to be patient. To show her that he'd meant it, every unspoken promise, every intense, loaded look, every casual brush of fingers that lingered a second too long to be merely friendly.

Kate Emerson had come crashing back into his life and James Nowak would be damned if he let her slip away again without a fight. This time, he'd prove to her that what they'd had was rare and precious and worth overcoming any obstacles for.

A Gathering Darkness

Kate was sorting through a bag of groceries when her phone rang. Startled, she reached for her phone, her pulse quickening as the caller ID displayed Thorek Hospital. With a swipe, she answered the call, pressing the phone to her ear as she tried to steady her nerves.

"Ms. Emerson? This is Nurse Patel." The voice on the other end was warm, a marked change from nurse she'd spoken to earlier. "I have good news. Your father's been moved to a private room. Visiting hours run until 8 PM, if you'd like to come see him."

Kate's stomach fluttered, a wave of relief washing over her, quickly followed by a surge of worry. "How is he? Any updates on his condition?"

A beat of hesitation. "I'm afraid I don't have any new information. But I know how anxious you've been to see him. He's in room 318 whenever you're ready."

"Thank you," Kate mumbled, ending the call and staring at the half-filled grocery bags scattered on the counter. The cottage cheese in her hand felt absurdly ordinary in the face of the news she'd just received. With a sigh, she quickly stored the perishables in the refrigerator, leaving the remaining groceries on the counter, forgotten for the moment.

She chose to walk, needing the physical act of movement to distract her from the turmoil within. The late afternoon sun filtered through the trees, casting dappled shadows on the sidewalk. With each step toward the hospital, a tightness gripped her chest, dread leaving a bitter taste in her mouth.

The moment Kate entered Walter's room, the sterile scent and rhythmic beeping overwhelmed her senses. Her father lay motionless, surrounded by medical equipment, his face pale against the hospital linens.

Moving as if through water, she approached the bed, the urge to turn and run battling with her desire to be close to him. Up close, his frailty was even more apparent, his skin so pale it seemed almost translucent. Hesitantly, she reached out to clasp his hand, alarmed by the unfamiliarity of its coolness.

"Dad," she whispered, her voice catching in her throat. "I'm here."

The sound of the door clicking open startled her, causing her heart to race. Dr. Phillips stood in the doorway, his face carefully composed, but his eyes held a depth of understanding and sympathy.

"Ms. Emerson. I wish we were meeting again under better circumstances." He motioned to the chair beside the bed. "May I?"

She could only nod, not trusting her voice. The doctor settled in the seat, hands clasped in front of him and forearms resting on his knees.

"As I mentioned yesterday, we believe your father suffered a massive stroke. The scans and tests we've run..." He paused, his gaze straying to Walter's lax face. "I'm so sorry, but the prognosis is grim."

The words reached Kate as if from underwater, warped and muffled. The room seemed to tilt on its axis, black spots crowding her vision.

"Walter is in what we call a persistent vegetative state," Dr.

Phillips continued gently. "The likelihood of him regaining consciousness is extremely low. And if he does, the brain damage is...significant. He would require round-the-clock care."

A high-pitched ringing arose in Kate's ears, nearly drowning out the doctor's next words.

"I know it's overwhelming to process. But we need to discuss your options moving forward. Keeping Walter on long-term life support is an expensive proposition, one not fully covered by his insurance..." He trailed off delicately.

The implication hung in the air, a sword of Damocles waiting to fall. Kate shook her head mutely, fingers digging into the plastic bed rail.

Dr. Phillips laid a hand on her arm, the warmth jarring against her icy skin. "You don't need to make any decisions now. Sleep on it, talk it over with your support system. I'm happy to put you in touch with the hospital counselors, if you think it would help."

Kate shook her head again, tears burning her eyes and closing her throat. The doctor smiled sadly, giving her arm a final gentle squeeze before standing.

"I'll check back in tomorrow, after we get the results of the latest neurological tests." He paused at the door, one hand on the knob. "Don't hesitate to have me paged if you need anything. And Ms. Emerson. I'm so very sorry."

Then he was gone and she was alone. Alone with the shell of her father and the impossible weight of his fate in her hands. A moan worked its way up from her chest, dragging with it great, heaving sobs that felt ripped from her very marrow.

Clutching Walter's limp hand in both of hers, Kate pressed her forehead to his knuckles, tears scalding her cheeks. "Dad, I'm sorry. I'm so sorry I wasn't here. I'm sorry I didn't call more or visit enough. I should've known you weren't okay, should've realized..."

The regrets spilled forth, each one leaving a bitter taste in her mouth. If only she'd been more attentive, more involved. Would it have changed anything? Logically, she understood that dwelling on hypotheticals was pointless, but that didn't stop them from echoing through her mind.

An abrupt tapping jolted her from her swirling thoughts, snapping her gaze toward the window. There, perched on the ledge, was a large crow, its black feathers contrasting with the pale moonlight. It stared at her with unnervingly intelligent eyes, head tilted, before pecking at the glass with a sound that echoed unsettlingly in the quiet room.

Gooseflesh rippled up Kate's arms, the fine hairs at her nape prickling. It had to be the same bird from the hospital parking garage the day before. What were the chances of—

Her thoughts were interrupted as she felt a faint pressure against her palm. Walter's fingers, barely moving, twitched slightly. Her heart leaped with a flicker of hope as she turned back to his face. But his eyes remained closed, his features still relaxed in the induced sleep.

The crow rapped against the window again, its persistence mirroring the subtle tightening of Walter's fingers around hers. Holding her breath, she leaned closer until her ear almost touched his dry, parched lips.

"Dad?" It was more breath than word. "Can you hear me?"

Time seemed to stretch, filled only with the rhythmic beep and whir of the machines, the rasp of Walter's assisted breathing. Then, a whisper, so soft she almost doubted her own ears, "Close..."

Kate recoiled in surprise, her eyes widening. Simultaneously, the crow unleashed a frantic flurry of pecks against the glass, and Walter's fingers tightened around hers in rhythm with the bird's assault. His grip was unexpectedly strong, squeezing her hand painfully.

She cried out in surprise and pain, reflexively trying to pull away. But just as suddenly as it had grasped her, Walter's hand went limp, falling back onto the blanket with a dull thud.

Her heart pounding, Kate spun toward the window. The crow was gone, leaving only a faint smudge on the glass and a lingering feeling of unease.

Her mind raced, synapses firing in rapid staccato as she tried to process the last few minutes. Had Walter really spoken? Had she hallucinated the crow, conjured it from her stress-fractured psyche? Some primitive part of her brain screamed that this was important somehow, that she ignore it at her peril.

Trembling, Kate gently disengaged her aching hand from Walter's limp grasp. She needed fresh air, needed to escape the heavy unease that filled the room. She stumbled toward the door, her fingers fumbling for the handle, a prickle of paranoia making her feel like she was being watched.

The corridor was a welcome relief, cool and well-lit after the oppressive quiet of the hospital room. Kate slid down the wall, feeling weak in the knees, and focused on controlling her breathing.

In. Out. In. Out.

The doctor's earlier words chose that moment to reassert themselves, a dull blade twisting under her ribs. She had to decide, is what it came down to. Pull the plug or watch Walter become a permanent vegetable, his continued survival a question mark dangling over her future.

How was she supposed to make that kind of call? What gave her the right to determine whether her father lived or died, tethered to machines in purgatory or free to move on to whatever waited after this mortal coil?

Kate pressed the heels of her hands to her burning eyes until kaleidoscopes of color burst behind the lids. She needed to get out of this place, away from the miasma of sickness and despair that coated her tongue, clogged her lungs.

With a deep breath, she pushed off the wall, her legs still unsteady. A final, lingering look at Walter's closed door brought a wave of regret, weighing heavily on her heart.

"I'll be back tomorrow," she promised in a thready whisper. "We'll figure this out."

Then, overwhelmed with a sense of inadequacy, she hurried away. Down the winding corridor, past the nurses' sympathetic glances, she pushed through the doors into the gathering dusk, seeking solace. Kate couldn't shake the feeling that she was escaping more than just the weighty decision looming over her.

That crow...and Walter's whispered word...

Close... he had said. *Close what? Close the door on any hope of her father's recovery? Close the door on their unfinished story, lose her last living link to a dwindling past?*

Kate shuddered, the balmy evening air suddenly cold as the grave. Somehow, she knew the crow's message wasn't about Walter at all. It was a warning, an omen of something far more sinister lurking on the horizon.

Something that had already slipped through an unguarded door, gaining ground with every minute she spent wrestling indecision.

And if she didn't find a way to close it...

Kate had a sinking suspicion it would be more than her father's life on the line. It would be her sanity, her very soul, sacrificed to whatever nightmares lived on the other side of that gaping portal.

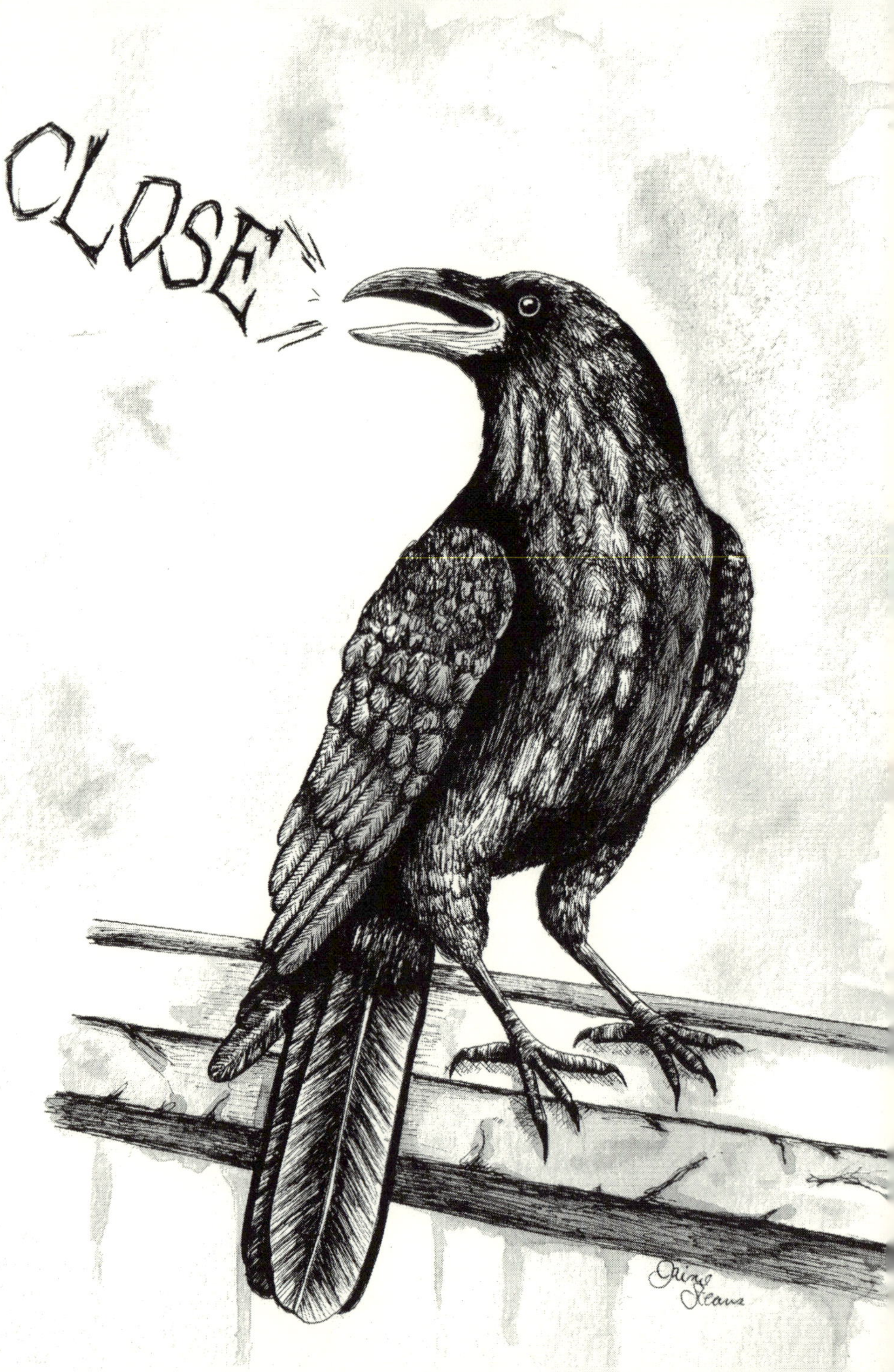
CLOSE

THE CROW'S OMEN

Kate stood in the hospital lobby, her dim reflection visible in the large windows that revealed the dark night outside that seemed to push against the glass, creating an unsettling atmosphere. A slight shiver ran through her. With an unsteady hand, she took out her phone and opened the Lyft app, her finger ready to request a ride.

After a moment's hesitation, she closed the app and retrieved the business card she had tucked into her pocket. With slightly trembling fingers, she dialed James's number and pressed the call button, her heartbeat quickening as she raised the phone to her ear.

"Hello?" James said, picking up the phone. The ambient noise of the busy cafe and bookstore could be heard in the background.

"Jimmy, hi," Kate replied, trying to keep her voice steady. "I'm at the hospital. I know it's late, and you're probably busy, but I was wondering if you could pick me up."

"Of course I can," he said, the response immediate. Kate smiled, picturing him already moving, keys in hand. "Which hospital are you at?"

"Thorek Memorial."

"On my way. I'll be there in about fifteen minutes."

"I'll be waiting in the lobby. Thank you, James. I really appreciate it."

"Don't worry about it," James assured her. "I'm on my way. Just sit tight, and I'll see you soon."

As the call ended, Kate felt a wave of relief wash over her. Knowing that James was coming to get her helped ease some of the tension that had built up inside her. She found a seat in the lobby and settled in to wait, her mind still grappling with the events that had brought her to the hospital in the first place.

True to his word, James's car glided to a stop outside the hospital entrance about fifteen minutes later. Kate slid into the passenger seat, sinking into the supple leather with a sigh. The air inside was warm, the faint scent of James's cologne both familiar and comforting. She felt some of the brittle tension begin to uncurl from her muscles as James pulled away from the curb, the hospital shrinking in the rearview mirror.

"Any news on Walter?" He glanced at her, then back at the road.

Kate responded with a slight shake of her head, her voice flat and unemotional. "Still in a coma. Nothing more than that."

"Sorry," James said, sensing her discomfort with talking about her father right now.

They drove in silence for a time, the only sounds the steady purr of the engine and the soft susurrus of tires on pavement. Kate let her gaze drift out the window, the blur of passing streetlights and shadowed buildings an almost hypnotic distraction from the clamor of her thoughts.

It wasn't until James turned onto a side street, the scenery shifting to quaint storefronts and cozy cafes, that Kate realized they weren't headed back to Walter's house. She glanced over at him, a question in the tilt of her head.

James offered a small, slightly sheepish smile in return. "I figured we could grab that coffee now, if you're feeling up to it," he explained, navigating the car into a spot outside The Caffeinated Page. The glow of the shop's windows cast his face in warm amber light, limning the angles and planes with soothing familiarity. "But if you'd rather just head home, say the word. No pressure."

For a long moment, Kate simply stared at him, throat working around the sudden upwelling of emotion. The casual thoughtfulness of the gesture, the way he'd anticipated her need for a buffer between the sterile chill of the hospital and the oppressive emptiness of her father's house...it struck her like a physical blow, a reminder of the steady, loyal kindness that had drawn her to him all those years ago.

"Coffee would be great, actually," she managed, a small, genuine smile finding its way to her lips. The thought of returning to the house, to the yawning silence and the reminders of her father's absence, sent a shudder rippling through her. No, she wasn't ready to face that particular echo chamber of grief quite yet. "Lead the way."

The rich, earthy scent of freshly ground beans embraced them as they stepped inside The Caffeinated Page, mingling with the low murmur of conversation and the whisper of turning pages. A scattering of patrons occupied the plush armchairs, sipping from mismatched ceramic mugs as they pored over their books or tapped away on sleek laptops. It felt like a separate world, a pocket of warmth and normalcy untouched by the tragedy that had subsumed Kate's life.

"Welcome to my little slice of heaven," James quipped, lips curling into a smile. He guided her to the polished oak counter where a fresh-faced barista was steaming milk with practiced flicks of her wrist, her bobbed hair a halo of purple ringlets.

"Emma, this is Kate, an old friend from high school. Kate, meet Emma, barista extraordinaire, book lover, and the first regular this place ever had." James's eyes crinkled at the corners as he tapped a knuckle on the counter in playful emphasis.

"Only regular, more like," Emma snorted, setting aside the milk pitcher to extend a hand to Kate. "Lovely to meet you! Any friend of Jimmy's, and all that." She winked, her grin impish. "Now, what can I get started for you two? Wait, let me guess—an extra-shot Americano for the boss man and..." She tapped a finger against pursed lips, hazel eyes narrowing speculatively. "A vanilla latte for the lady?"

Surprised laughter bubbled up Kate's throat. "Impressive. I'll take that latte, thanks."

Orders placed, James ushered Kate to a table by the front window, the warm honey color of the reclaimed wood gleaming under the pendant lamps. As Emma worked her magic behind the bar, he regaled Kate with the tale of how The Caffeinated Page came to be.

"I bought the shop not long after I got out of the Army," he said, his fingers toying with a stray napkin. "It was just a hole-in-the-wall secondhand bookstore then, barely scraping by. I used my VA loan to expand and add the café." His eyes softened with memory. "Em was my only regular at first, before the renovations. She'd camp out for hours reading a book she never bought and sipping from this huge thermos of home-brewed coffee. That's what gave me the idea to add the espresso bar, actually."

"Your Manic Pixie Dream Barista," Kate teased, an eyebrow arched, " inspiring you to follow your bliss?"

James's startled laugh was a warm burst of sound. "I can always trust you to call me on my cliches." His eyes danced as Emma delivered their drinks with a flourish. "I'm a walking trope. Kid from the wrong side of the tracks, barely graduated from high school, enlisted in the Army to escape the streets…" He trailed off, a shadow flickering across his face. Shaking it off, he half-smiled at Kate. "But what about you, Counselor? Word on the street is that you're a rising star in the legal world."

Kate demurred with a wave of her hand, but obliged, filling him in on law school in LA, passing the bar, landing her dream job at a prestigious firm. They sipped and talked, marveling at the twists of fate that had brought them from the halls of Lake View High to this quiet tête-à-tête in a cozy neighborhood café.

"Do you stay in contact with anyone from the old gang?"

James asked, studying her over the rim of his mug. "From back in the day?"

Something painful spasmed across Kate's face before she caught it, smoothing her expression into careful neutrality. "No, not really. When I left for California, I pretty much put Chicago in the rear view. Haven't been back since my mom..." Her throat worked around the words that wouldn't come.

James made a soft, wounded noise, setting his cup down with a muted clink. "Yeah, so sorry, Kate...my mom wrote to me about Eleanor's accident while I was deployed. I am so sorry I wasn't here for you." His hands twitched as he continued to tear at the napkin, as if fighting the urge to reach for her.

Kate nodded, struggling to maintain her composure. "Thank you." A profound sense of guilt began to consume her, stemming from her prolonged absence and the emotional chasm that had developed between her and Walter. Hesitantly, she shared the details of her father's health status with James, relaying the physicians' grim outlook and the daunting choice she would soon need to make.

He listened, a furrow carved between his brows and a muscle ticking in his jaw. When she finished, he did reach out, his hand warm and solid as it engulfed her own.

"Jesus, Kate. That's... I am so goddamn sorry. I can't imagine what you must be feeling." His thumb traced soothing circles over her knuckles, as if he could leach the hurt from her through that simple touch. "If there's anything, and I mean anything, I can do..."

"I appreciate that." Kate attempted a smile as she gently extricated her hand, instantly missing the grounding weight of his touch. An awkward beat passed, the air suddenly too thick, the unspoken history between them a presence in itself.

Fixing her gaze on a fascinating swirl in the wood grain of the table, Kate forced a lightness into her voice that she didn't feel. "I should probably call it a night. Lots of heavy thoughts to wrestle to the ground." She pushed back her chair with a scrape, wincing at the harsh sound.

James got to his feet. "Right, of course. Let me drive you." He caught Emma's eye over Kate's shoulder, nodding his head in the direction of the exit, conveying his intentions without words. Emma flashed him a thumbs up in response before turning to greet the next customer.

The ride back to Walter's house passed in heavy silence, both of them wrapped in their own turbulent thoughts. James guided the sedan to a smooth stop alongside the curb, prompting Kate to shift her gaze toward him, her eyes glistening with the unmistakable presence of welling emotion.

"Thank you, Jimmy. For the ride, the coffee, the shoulder." She reached out to grip his forearm, lips trembling with the effort of holding back the deluge. "It means... God, it means everything to have a friendly face from the past surface in the middle of this nightmare."

He covered her hand with his own, fingertips resting on

the rabbit-quick throb of her pulse. "I'm here, Kate. Whatever you need, whenever you need it. I hope you know that."

She dredged up a smile that felt too tight, too brittle. Then, before she could second-guess the impulse, she leaned across the center console to wrap her arms around his shoulders. For one suspended moment, they clung to each other, breathing in the scent of shared history and old heartache. James's cologne—the same scent he'd favored in high school—enveloped her, stirring up a bittersweet tide of memory.

Drawing in an unsteady breath, Kate pulled back, cheeks damp. With a final squeeze of his arm, she slid out of the car and marched up the front walk, the soles of her shoes unnaturally loud against the concrete. At the door, she turned to lift a hand in farewell, watching until James's tail lights disappeared around the corner and she was alone.

The house crouched dark and silent before her, windows blank as shuttered eyes. Kate hesitated on the threshold, key hovering an inch from the lock. An unnameable dread crept up her spine, raising fine hairs on her arms and the back of her neck. Shaking it off with an irritated huff, she jammed the key home, the click of the tumblers ominous in the uncertain gloom.

A shaking hand groped for the light switch as the door swung open but before Kate's searching fingers found purchase, a flicker of movement in the darkened living room froze her in place.

There, perched on the back of Walter's favorite armchair

like a raven heralding ill-tidings, was the crow from the hospital. It cocked its head, glittering beetle-black eyes boring into Kate's as if peering into the most sheltered chambers of her heart.

Then, with a harsh, rasping caw—a sound that held far too much intelligence, far too much sly malice to be merely animal—it spoke a single, damning word.

"Close."

The oily syllable shivered through the room, echoing off the walls and burrowing under Kate's skin like a parasite. She blinked, lids slamming down on suddenly burning eyes—

—and in that split second of blindness, the bird vanished. Between one heartbeat and the next, there was only a single ebony feather left behind on the faded print of the armchair.

With a strangled gasp, Kate flipped on the light, bathing the room in a weak amber wash that did nothing to dispel the clammy tendrils of unease coiling in her belly. Hands shaking, she crossed the room to pluck the feather from the upholstery, twirling it between numb fingers as if it might hold the answers to the impossible questions crowding her skull.

All this shit made absolutely no sense. Fragmented images swirled through Kate's mind, a dizzying kaleidoscope of horror: her father, wasted and unresponsive, tethered to a hospital bed; the half-finished painting in the upstairs studio, its faceless subject and the sinister figure that lurked in its pigment; the unearthly, knowing glimmer in a beady avian eye...

An icy gust of wind stirred the curtains, carrying on its current a stomach-churning whiff of decay and sickly-sweet rot. Kate spun on her heel, heart clawing its way up her throat, but she was alone. The room lay undisturbed, mocking in its veneer of normalcy.

Only... it wasn't quite empty, was it? A presence, unseen but unmistakably felt, hung heavy in the air, curdling on Kate's tongue and prickling along her skin. She had the sudden, unshakable sense of being watched, stalked, sized up by some voracious entity licking its chops at the thought of sinking in its teeth.

The crow's ominous decree—*"Close"*—snarled through her head in an endless, taunting loop, stoking her already frayed nerves to new heights of agitation. But close what? And why did some primal, lizard-brain part of her tremble at the very idea of unearthing that secret?

Her father's bruised and papery face drifted across her mind's eye, and Kate shuddered. Icy talons squeezed her heart, a monstrous weight settling on her chest until she could scarcely draw breath. The temptation to flee this house, this block, this whole damned city sang in her blood, urging her to run until Chicago was nothing but a bad memory fading in the rearview.

But she couldn't abandon her post, not now, not with Walter's very life hanging in the balance. No. Whatever vicious force had staged this home invasion, whatever noxious truths lurked behind its subterfuge... Kate would just have to grit her teeth and face them down. For her father, for herself, for the chance to look her own reflection in the eye without flinching. She would stand her ground against the dark. Even if it cost her everything.

With a breath that shook like brittle leaves in an October gale, Kate tightened her grip on the feather, its barb biting into the thin skin of her palm. She straightened her spine, tipped up her chin, and stared into the yawning shadows with a defiance she didn't truly feel.

"Okay, you bastards," she whispered, a prayer and a curse. "I'm here. Show me what you've got."

Only silence, thick and treacly as old blood, answered. But Kate knew, soul-deep, that this was merely the calm before the storm. That whatever waited in the wings was simply biding its time, gathering its strength.

And when it finally stepped into the light and showed its true face...Heaven help her, because Kate had a feeling that nothing on this mortal earth would be up to the job. All she could do was dig in her heels, clench her jaw until her teeth ached, and pray she was ready for the devils to come.

Even as a small, sniveling voice in the back of her head whispered that no one, least of all her, could ever be ready for the kind of nightmares she'd unwittingly invited in. But there could be no retreat now. The battle lines had been drawn. It was time to see just what sort of mettle Kate Emerson was made of.

A Grim Prognosis

Kate sat stiffly in the small meeting room, hands clasped tightly together in her lap, the tension causing her knuckles to pale. James sat beside her, his steady, reassuring presence providing a measure of comfort against the turmoil of feelings roiling inside her. The fluorescent overhead lighting created sharp-edged shadows on the synthetic tabletop, and the atmosphere felt heavy, almost palpably so, with the anticipation of imminent bad news.

The door swung open on nearly silent hinges, admitting Dr. Phillips. His kind face was drawn, etched with lines of exhaustion and empathy in equal measure. Settling into the seat across from them, he steepled his fingers and met Kate's gaze head-on.

"Kate, I'm so very sorry, but I'm afraid I have difficult news regarding your father's condition."

Though she'd known it was coming, had tried to brace for the blow, the words still slammed into Kate like a physical thing, driving the breath from her lungs and sending icy dread percolating into her marrow. Mute, she dipped her chin in acknowledgment, not trusting the steadiness of her voice.

Dr. Phillips gentled his tone but maintained the crisp professionalism of a seasoned bearer of bad tidings. "As we discussed previously, the stroke Walter suffered caused significant damage to his brain. We've conducted a comprehensive battery of diagnostic tests to assess the extent and implications of his injury."

He enumerated the procedures in detail—neurological exams, CT scans, MRIs, EEGs. Each one a brush stroke in the bleak portrait of Walter's prognosis. The medical jargon washed over Kate in a disorienting deluge, her mind flailing to process, to paint a picture of the half-life that yawned before her father.

"I'm so sorry to have to tell you this," Dr. Phillips continued, genuine regret softening his features, "but the results indicate widespread, irreversible damage. Walter's brain function is so severely compromised that he will not be able to regain consciousness or maintain essential physiological processes without artificial support."

The room tilted, warped, the ugly beige carpet dropping out from beneath Kate's feet. She was plummeting in free fall, scrambling desperately for a handhold, an anchor, anything to arrest her dizzying plunge into this waking nightmare.

Then James's hand found hers under the table, his rough palm enveloping her fingers, grounding her with the familiar warmth of his skin. Their digits laced, twined, fused, a silent declaration of solidarity in the face of unimaginable grief.

"I recognize how incredibly difficult this is to hear, to process," Dr. Phillips offered, "but it's vitally important that you begin considering the next steps in Walter's care. Given his current status and the grim prospect of recovery, it may be time to have a frank discussion about withdrawing life-sustaining interventions."

The doctor's words cracked across Kate's psyche like a whip, flaying her open and exposing the raw, pulsing ugliness of reality. James, seated next to her, stiffened abruptly, a quick, audible breath drawn in through clenched teeth as his hand clamped around hers with an almost painful intensity.

"I know it feels impossibly cruel to even contemplate," Dr. Phillips hurried to add, as if sensing the violent rejection of the very notion radiating from them in waves. "Please believe me when I say that no one would ask this of you lightly. But these are the hard questions we must grapple with now. What would Walter want, if he could speak for himself? What path forward honors his values, preserves his dignity, saves him from needless suffering?"

As Kate sat there, vivid recollections assailed her without warning, leaving her momentarily disoriented. She remembered Walter, vibrant and healthy, his eyes alight with playfulness as he patiently showed her how to hold a fishing rod, use a turntable, and grip a car's steering wheel. Those images then shifted to Walter after her mother passed, a man diminished and apathetic, navigating an existence that seemed leached of color, happiness, and purpose. Kate attempted to picture him confined to the restrictive hospital bed, reliant on machines to breathe, untethered and adrift, but found to her dismay that she struggled to form a distinct mental image. Doubts began to gnaw at her. Did she genuinely understand what he would have desired if their circumstances were reversed? That troubling question opened up within her like a widening chasm, leaving her feeling profoundly unsettled and adrift in a sea of uncertainty.

"Of course, you don't need to decide anything right now,"

THE DEVIL'S DOORWAY

Dr. Phillips assured, rising from his chair and drifting toward the door. "Our team will provide you with all the information and support you need to help guide you through this impossible situation."

He paused at the threshold, one hand on the knob, and turned back. The harsh light picked out the silver at his temples, the deep grooves bracketing his mouth. In that instant, he seemed impossibly old and impossibly sad.

"For whatever little it's worth... I am so very sorry, Ms. Emerson."

Then he was gone, leaving nothing but antiseptic air and deafening silence in his wake. For a long, suspended moment, Kate simply stared at the closed door, unblinking. She wasn't sure what finally shattered her fragile composure—the squeak of James's chair as he shifted closer, the soft exhalation of his breath in the too-quiet room, or perhaps the intangible, inexorable tug of a lifetime of love and loss and unspoken goodbyes.

But shatter she did.

The first sob tore loose from her chest, jagged and brutal. It was the key that unlocked the floodgates, unleashing a deluge of primal, wordless anguish that burst past her gritted teeth and trembling lips. The force of it bent her double, drove her face into her hands as if she could somehow hide from the howling abyss rending her heart in two.

Dimly, she registered James's arms coming around her, tentative at first, then fierce, crushing her to his chest as if he could absorb her agony through sheer force of will. Hot tears dripped into her hair, salt and copper on her tongue, and she realized distantly that he was weeping too, his elegant fingers clutching at her shoulders, her back, scrabbling for purchase against the riptide of misery intent on dragging them both under.

He was murmuring something—maybe her name, maybe platitudes, maybe prayers to a god neither of them had ever really believed in. It didn't matter; the words were a meaningless buzz, white noise against the roar of her pulse in her ears. There was only the warm, solid wall of him, the scent of his skin, the hitching rise and fall of his chest, and even that was just a temporary harbor, a bit of flotsam to cling to as the tempest raged on.

Kate had no concept of how long they huddled there, fused together in that sterile room with its limp plastic ficus and its eggshell walls that had borne witness to so much despair. Gradually, like a tide receding by inches from a battered shore, the explosion of grief gentled, quieted, transmuted into a yawning numbness too profound for tears. She drew back from the shelter of James's arms, swiping at her ravaged face with the back of one trembling hand.

"I don't... Jimmy, what do I do?" she asked, her voice hoarse and strained from emotion. "How can I possibly make this choice on my own?"

She looked to Jimmy, hoping for guidance or reassurance, some indication of what the right path forward might be. But deep down, she knew that this was a choice only she could make, as daunting and solitary as that felt.

James's hands came up to cradle her jaw, tilting her chin so he could meet her gaze head-on. His eyes were red-rimmed and swollen, the warm brown swamped by the same lost, frightened desolation she knew must be mirrored in her own.

"You listen to me, Kate Emerson," he said, low and fierce. "You are not alone in this. Not now, not ever. I am here, right by your side, come hell or high water. We will bear this together, and we will figure out the way forward together. You don't have to carry this alone."

She felt something give way inside her at his words, not breaking, but shifting, like a joint popping back into its proper place. Raising her own hands to cover his where they still framed her face, she nodded, the movement jerky but resolute.

"Okay," she breathed, little more than a sigh. Leaning forward until her forehead rested against his, she let her eyes flutter closed, just for a moment. "Okay."

Drawing a shuddering breath from some untapped wellspring of strength, Kate sat back, spine stiffening with renewed conviction. When she met James's eyes this time, her own were clearer, steadier, alight with grim determination.

"I need to see him. I can't... I won't make any decisions until I've looked him in the eye and done my best to discern his wishes. I owe him that much."

James's hands fell to her shoulders, pride and tenderness

and old sorrow mingling in his gaze. "Of course. Take all the time you need. I'll be right outside if you want me."

She managed a smile, tiny and wobbly, but genuine. "I always want you, Jimmy Nowak. But I think... I think this is something I need to do on my own. At least at first."

He accepted this with a brush of his lips against her forehead, there and gone like a whisper. Then he was rising, tugging her to her feet and steadying her when she swayed. Together, they made their way out of the conference room and down the winding maze of corridors, their footsteps a muffled metronome in the muted bustle of the ward.

All too soon, they stood outside the closed door to Walter's room. Through the wood, Kate could hear the now-familiar chorus of mechanized life—the hiss of the ventilator, the steady beep of the heart monitor, the whoosh of the blood pressure cuff. Such cold comfort, those impersonal sounds, a stark reminder of all that hung in the balance.

Her hand shook as she reached for the knob, a hairline tremble she couldn't quite quell. Beside her, James shifted, an aborted movement, as if he'd begun to reach for her before thinking better of it. She felt his eyes on her, solemn, searching, silently beseeching. With an unsteady exhale, she twisted the handle and stepped across the threshold into the dimness beyond.

The door clicked shut behind her with a muffled finality, and Kate was alone, alone with the shell of her father, with the weight of an impossible goodbye, with the looming specter of a choice that would cleave her life into before and after.

Sinking into the chair at Walter's bedside, she reached for his lax fingers, trying not to flinch at their waxy, unfamiliar coolness. Bowing her head as if in prayer, she brought his hand to her lips, choking on a fresh wave of tears as the salt of her grief mixed with the copper-bright tang of sorrow on her tongue.

"Hey, Daddy," she whispered, the childhood endearment rusty and bittersweet. "It's me. It's Katie-bird. I'm here."

In the ensuing silence, broken only by the soulless drone of machines playing at life, one thought tolled through her head, clanging like a funeral bell. Nothing would ever be the same.

A Canvas of Horrors

I n the days that followed, Kate moved through a fog of subdued grief, constantly aware of the inescapable decision she would soon have to make. She spent most of her time next to Walter's hospital bed, her eyes fixed on his expressionless, motionless face, which stood in clear contrast to the machines around him that beeped and whirred, mechanical proof of life that surrounded him.

She clung to his limp hand with a desperate ferocity, searching for any flicker, any sign of the vibrant, steady presence that had anchored her world for as long as she could remember. But there was only the waxy coolness of his skin, the soulless metronome of the monitors, the discordant hiss and click of the ventilator. All of it a macabre reminder that the essence of the man—the warmth, the wisdom, the quiet strength—had already slipped beyond reach.

In the depths of her being, in a place untouched by shock or sentiment, Kate understood with a sickening certainty that this was not what Walter would want. Her father had always been a force of nature, a man who moved through life with purpose and determination. To see him reduced to this—a husk tethered to machines, suspended between worlds—was an affront to everything he'd held sacred. She knew, with a clarity sharper than scalpels, that to keep him trapped in this limbo would be the ultimate betrayal, a fate crueler than the most brutal death.

And yet, the weight of that knowledge, the sheer enormity of the power to make that final determination, threatened to crush Kate beneath its mass. As an only child, she'd always shouldered the mantle of responsibility, but this went beyond anything she'd ever imagined. With her mother gone and her father's sister hundreds of miles away, lost in her own haze of rural Nebraska, there was no one to share the burden, no one to absolve Kate of the choice that would end one life and shatter another.

Guilt and doubt entwined in a sickening spiral, twisting Kate's insides until she was sure she'd crumble beneath the strain. How dare she even contemplate such a thing? How could she look at the face that had gazed at her with such love, such pride, and coolly, clinically, sign his death warrant? What right did she have to play God, to extinguish the flame that had lit her way in the darkness for longer than memory?

But even as those questions scoured her raw, Kate knew, in the secret chambers of her heart, what had to be done. And so, with shaking hands and unshed tears, she called the doctor into Walter's room and laid her burden at his feet. The words tasted of ash and betrayal, but she forced them out, each one a shard of glass in her throat.

They set the time for the next evening, a cold, impersonal formality that stood in obscene contrast to the visceral, world-ending reality of what was to come. Kate nodded along numbly to the logistics, the banalities of paperwork and procedure, feeling as if she were watching herself from a vast distance, an unwilling spectator to her own unraveling.

That night, she called James. Grief this profound demanded witness, craved the soothing balm of shared sorrow and steadying hands. He answered on the first ring, his voice low and soft with unspoken understanding. In halting, tear-strangled increments, Kate laid herself bare—the decision, the appointment, the yawning chasm of loss that threatened to devour her whole.

Not once did he offer platitudes or hollow comfort. He simply listened, his breathing a soothing metronome in her ear. And when she'd poured out the last bitter dregs of her anguish, he said simply, "I'll be there, Kate. You don't have to do this alone."

Promises to pick her up an hour before the scheduled time and soft, gruff words of comfort were the last things Kate remembered before exhaustion claimed her, dragging her down into the restless oblivion of a grief-soaked sleep.

That night, the dreams returned with a vengeance, twisted cinema reels of horror projected on the backs of her eyelids. Walter's face loomed before her, contorted in terror and desperation. His voice, raw and urgent, scraped across her subconscious like barbed wire.

"Close the door, Katie-bird! Time's running out...once I'm gone, there'll be nothing holding it back. You have to find a way to lock it down, to sever the link. Before it's too late!"

And always, always, the shadow figure lurked at the edges of her vision, a malevolent silhouette pulsing with hunger. With each of Walter's pleas, it seemed to grow, to swell, an ugly boil gorged on fear and despair. In the final, terrible moments before waking, it surged forward in a tsunami of darkness, engulfing father and daughter alike in its ravenous, grasping maw.

Kate jackknifed upright with a breathless scream, the echoes of the nightmare still clinging to her sweat-slicked skin. Heart galloping behind her ribs, she stared wildly into the gloom of the living room.

A sudden crack shattered the predawn hush, sending Kate scrambling at the sheet, damp cotton bunching beneath seeking fingers. She knew that sound, had heard it countless times over long, scorching summers. The distinctive pop of aged wood losing its battle with humidity and heat, finally surrendering to the forces of nature and time.

But this...this was different, sharper, almost deliberately jarring. It dragged Kate from the sofa on wobbly legs, pulled her inexorably up the stairs and down the shadowed hall to the one place she couldn't bear to look.

Walter's studio door gaped like a wound, the darkness beyond fathomless and unfamiliar. Fighting the urge to gag on the sudden cloying stench—spoiled fruit and something fouler, something that conjured images of fresh blood and ancient tombs—Kate fumbled for the light switch, each labored breath sawing at her lungs.

The meager light revealed a scene of subtle chaos. Crumpled tubes of paint, crusted brushes, and an avalanche of loose paper littered the floor, scattered outward from the easel like debris flung from the epicenter of some tiny, cataclysmic explosion. And there, glaring up at her from the midst of the carnage like a cracked and accusing eye, was the Ouija board.

Even from across the room, Kate could see that it wasn't where she'd left it.

Gooseflesh erupted down her arms in a fell wave as she crossed the small space, each step leaden with dread. Bending, Kate retrieved the board, setting it with exaggerated care on the paint-spattered desk. Its weight in her palms was at once utterly mundane and obscenely wrong, cold and unyielding beneath her fingertips.

A flicker of movement in her peripheral vision wrenched Kate's attention to the easel. Or rather, to the canvas propped upon it, the faceless portrait whose static menace hadn't diminished one iota in the intervening days. If anything, its aura of skewed wrongness had only intensified, an almost perceptible miasma that coated the back of Kate's throat like rancid syrup.

But it wasn't just atmosphere fueling the sudden spike of her terror. No, this was tangible, physical, a violation so profound it stole the breath from her lungs and the strength from her knees.

There, protruding from the dead center of the unfinished figure of the woman like an obscene dart, was the Ouija board's planchette. The impact had split the canvas in a jagged gash, rending the faceless woman nearly in two. From her position by the desk, Kate saw the exposed skeleton of stretcher bars, the ugly fissure gaping like a wound that would never heal.

"What the fuck..." she breathed, the words thin and bloodless in the oppressive air. On wooden legs, she drifted closer to the desecrated painting, one hand outstretched in morbid fascination. Curling numb fingers around the planchette's cool, curved edge, she wrenched it free in a single violent motion.

The void left behind pulsed with an oily, devouring blackness, a darkness that defied the room's weak light. It almost seemed to reach for Kate, to strain against the bonds of paint and primed linen, to hunger. For her.

Bile scalded the back of her throat as the planchette trembled between her fingers, suddenly too heavy to hold. Without thought, responding to some base, inscrutable instinct, Kate raised the filigreed lens of its aperture to her eye, the curve of it kissing her cheek..

The effect was instantaneous and horrifying. Superimposed over the ruin of the portrait like a photographic negative was the shadow figure of her nightmares. Tall and preternaturally thin, it loomed behind the painted woman, one long-fingered hand splayed across her chest in a gesture that was both intimate and profane. The place where its touch fell was a livid, coruscating orange-red, a pestilential glow that smoked and pulsated with its own diseased rhythm.

As Kate watched in mute, paralytic terror, the thing began to move. Sinuous as hissing eels, its lower limbs flexed and extended, sliding through the gash in the canvas in a grotesque parody of breech birth. The lurid light limned each contortion, each unnatural ripple and flex, until Kate was certain she could smell the charred meat reek of it, could feel the blistering heat of its passage.

With a ragged cry, she flung the planchette away, reeling back on unsteady feet. The wooden disk hit the floor with a clatter, skittering away under the table, but Kate barely registered the sound over the thunder of blood in her ears. Tearing her gaze from the violated painting, she stumbled for the door on legs that threatened to buckle, one hand clamped tight over her mouth lest the scream building in her chest rip free and shatter her.

Wrenching the door shut behind her with enough force to set the hinges groaning, Kate collapsed against it, her heartbeat a wild, trapped thing behind the cage of her ribs. She slid to the cool hardwood of the hall, knees pulled tight to her chest, eyes wide and staring into the gloom as if the horrors of the studio might ooze through the barricade of the door and infect the rest of the house with their poison.

But as the first weak rays of dawn crept across the floor and Kate's breathing gradually slowed from panicked gasps to a steadier rhythm, a grim realization settled in her churning gut. The nightmare made manifest in Walter's studio, the Ouija board and its impossible trajectory, the feel of the shadow figure's grasping hands reaching out from the depths of the painting...as terrifying as it all was, it paled in comparison to the ordeal that lay ahead.

For in the sober light of day, stripped of the hallucinogenic sheen of darkness and dread, Kate knew the true horror still awaited her. In a sterile hospital room across town, her father lay suspended in a purgatory of wires and tubes, his life—and death—bound inextricably to the machines that sustained his dwindling shell. And in a few short hours, Kate would enter that room one last time to say a goodbye that would cleave her world in two.

Curled against the unyielding floor, drained and raw and utterly heartsick, she let the tears come. Great, racking sobs that felt ripped from some primal, howling place, the anguish of an orphaned child and a grieving daughter given voice at last. She cried for her father, for herself, for the yawning void of loss and loneliness that waited on the other side of this unimaginable day.

But most of all, Kate wept for the growing certainty that this—this vigil of sorrow and dread—was merely the opening salvo in a war she hadn't known she was drafted to fight. That the shadow figure and its malevolent promise, the disjointed warnings torn from Walter's ruined brain, were but heralds of a greater darkness to come. A darkness she would soon face alone, the last soldier standing against the dying of the light.

With salt on her lips and lead in her limbs, Kate pushed to her feet, spine stiffening with grim resolve. For better or worse, in sickness and health, she had a promise to keep.

PART TWO

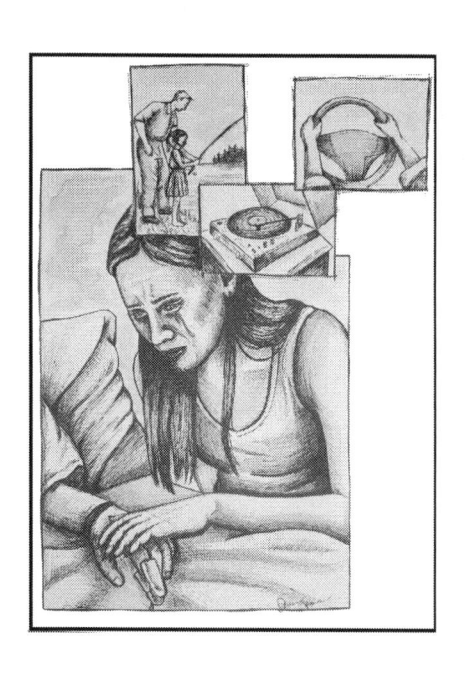

REQUIEM FOR WALTER

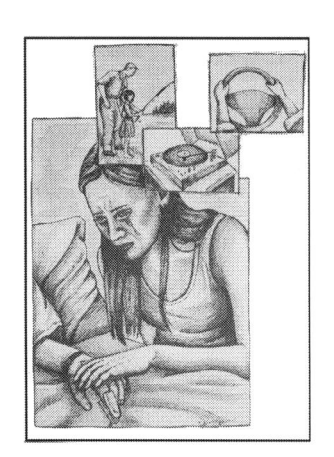

Morning dawned gray and bleak, the sky a leaden weight pressing down on Kate's shoulders as she sat on the porch steps, hands clasped tightly in her lap. The crunch of tires on gravel announced James's arrival, but she couldn't muster the energy to stand, to paste on a brave face and pretend that her world wasn't crumbling to ash.

He was out of the car in an instant, long legs eating up the distance between them. One look at her face, at the dark smudges beneath haunted eyes, and he was dropping to his knees before her, warm hands engulfing her own.

"Kate? What is it, what's happened?" The words were gentle, but beneath them thrummed an undercurrent of urgency, of tightly leashed fear.

She swallowed hard, tongue darting out to wet cracked lips. "Before we go...there's something I need to show you. Inside."

James hesitated, confusion clashing with concern in his mahogany eyes. But he didn't argue, just nodded and straightened, offering a hand to help her to her feet. Kate let him pull her up, let the steadying warmth of his touch anchor her as she led him into the house and up the stairs, each step heavier than the last.

At the threshold of Walter's studio, she paused, hand trembling on the doorknob. James shifted behind her, an unmistakable presence at her back, and she drew in a shaky breath, bolstered by his unwavering support. With a twist of her wrist, she pushed the door open and stepped inside.

She heard James's sharp intake of breath, felt the sudden tension in his frame as he took in the repurposed space, the easel and canvases and drifts of sketches littering every surface. But she didn't turn, didn't acknowledge his unspoken questions. Instead, she drifted to the painting that had haunted her waking dreams, the faceless woman—Eleanor, her mother—forever trapped in two dimensions.

"I wanted you to see *this*," she said, voice hardly more than a whisper. One trembling finger traced the air above the vicious gash in the canvas, the wound that had wept shadow and malice. "Do you...can you see anything behind her? In the tear?"

James stepped closer, brow furrowed. He studied the painting for a long moment, head tilted, before shaking his head slowly. "I see a park, trees, the usual background details. But nothing unusual. Why, what do you see?"

Kate shuddered, a full-body ripple of unease. "And no...no figures? No shadow lurking behind her?"

His frown deepened, worry etching itself into the lines of his face. "No, nothing like that. Kate, what's going on?"

But she was already moving past him, feet carrying her to the paint-splattered desk as if of their own volition. On her knee, with hands that shook only slightly, she fished the planchette out from under table where it had skittered after she dropped it in the early morning hours, the dull sheen of its lens winking at her like a blind eye.

"I found this the other day. Here, in Dad's studio." She turned to face James, the planchette light but significant in her cupped palms. "He had a Ouija board, Jimmy. Him, of all people."

James blinked, nonplussed. "Walter? But he's not...I mean,

he always seemed so rational. Grounded. I never would've pegged him for the type to mess around with that stuff."

"He's not," Kate said emphatically. "He doesn't believe in the occult or the supernatural or life after death. So explain this." She thrust the planchette at James, the movement almost violent in its intensity.

He took it gingerly, as if afraid it might bite. The whorls and eddies of the wood grain stood out against his fingers, the crystal of the viewing window cold and unyielding.

Kate nodded at it, a sharp jerk of her chin. "Hold it up to your eye. Look through the lens and tell me what you see."

James hesitated, a muscle ticking in his jaw. But he did as she asked, raising the planchette until it rested against his cheekbone, his gaze skimming the ruined painting once more.

"I see the same thing," he said after a moment, lowering his hand. "The portrait, the background. Nothing's changed."

Disappointment welled in Kate's gut, hot and coppery. Some small, secret part of her had hoped... But no. Of course James couldn't see the horrors that lurked just beyond the veil of normalcy. Why would he be party to her own private descent into madness?

Wordlessly, she took the planchette from his unresisting fingers, holding it up to her own eye with a kind of grim resignation. But the scene remained unchanged—no looming specter, no glowing fissure. Just paint and canvas and the sour taste of frustration on her tongue.

"Kate." James's voice was soft, almost unbearably gentle. "Please, talk to me. What's really going on here?"

The urge to speak grew stronger, the unspoken words struggling to break free from where they had lodged themselves inside her throat. It was a physical sensation, an insistent pressure that built with each passing moment she held them back. She could feel them there, a palpable presence demanding to be given voice, straining against her reluctance to let them out into the world.

The disturbing dreams, the unsettling artwork, the reaching hands of the shadowy being, and her dad's enigmatic cautions all lingered at the forefront of her thoughts. Kate felt the urge to let it all pour out in a flood of words, to give voice to these experiences that strained the bounds of credibility. Yet she hesitated, the extraordinary nature of it all holding her back as the words waited, poised on the very edge of expression.

Just as the words were about to take shape, the alarm on her phone chimed, interrupting the moment and bringing their attention back to the unpleasant job that lay ahead. The sudden noise cut through the tentative atmosphere like a knife, preventing the delicate threads of admission from fully materializing.

"We have to go," Kate said abruptly, turning on her heel. "I can't...we don't have time for this right now."

But James's hand on her wrist stopped her short, his touch

searing even through the thin barrier of her sleeve. "Kate. Please."

Kate avoided looking directly at him, unwilling to witness the worry and bewilderment she was certain his gaze held. But she owed him something, some scrap of truth to cling to in the coming tempest.

"I promise, I'll explain everything later. After..." She swallowed hard, forcing the words past the sudden knot in her throat. "After we say goodbye. I just...I need you to trust me right now, Jimmy. Can you do that?"

The pause that followed was agonizing, an eternity condensed into a handful of heartbeats. But then James was nodding, his grip on her arm tightening fractionally before falling away.

"Of course. Always." The words were low and fierce vow. "I'm here, Kate. No matter what."

She managed a jerky nod, not trusting herself to speak past the sudden upwelling of emotion. His unwavering faith, his steadfast loyalty in the face of her reticence...it was a solace and a struggle, a promise she wasn't sure she could keep.

But there would be time for explanations later, for confessions whispered in the dark. For now, they had a duty to fulfill, a farewell to make. And so, with a final glance at the painting that had become the axis around which her nightmare world spun, Kate squared her shoulders and walked out of the studio, James a silent shadow at her heels.

The drive to the hospital was a blur, a smear of gray sky and damp streets. Kate sat rigid in the passenger seat, fingers knotted in her lap as she stared unseeing out the window. Beside her, James was a steady presence, his hands sure on the wheel, his breathing even and measured. She drew strength from his composure, from the unspoken assurance that he would be her rock, her anchor in the storm to come.

All too soon, they were pulling into the hospital parking lot, the imposing brick edifice looming above them like a mausoleum. Kate's legs felt rubbery, insubstantial, as she climbed out of the car, each step toward the entrance a Herculean effort. But James was there, his hand finding hers, his fingers lacing through her own as they crossed the threshold into the sterile, antiseptic world beyond.

The walk to Walter's room was an eternity compressed into a handful of minutes, a surreal blur of fluorescent lights and hushed voices and the acrid tang of sickness. By the time they reached the door, Kate's heart was a wild thing battering itself against the cage of her ribs, a trapped bird desperate for release.

But there could be no turning back, no last-minute reprieve. With a deep breath that shuddered in her lungs,

Kate pushed down on the handle and stepped inside, James, a reliable presence bolstering her.

The room was dim, lit only by the soft glow of the monitors and the weak gray light filtering through the window. And there, in the center of it all, lay Walter, wasting and still, a husk tethered to a spider's web of wires and tubes. The ventilator clicked and hissed, a mechanical metronome measuring out the last beats of a life nearly spent.

Kate's throat closed, unshed tears scalding the backs of her eyes. She drifted to the bed as if in a trance, sinking into the chair at her father's side. With hands that trembled only slightly, she reached out to clasp his limp fingers, the papery skin cool and dry against her own.

"I'm here, Dad," she whispered, the words cracking and breaking on her tongue. "I'm here, and I...I'm so sorry."

Sorry for not being there, for not seeing the signs. Sorry for the years of distance, for the unspoken words and missed chances. Sorry for the choice I have to make, the terrible responsibility of holding your life in my faltering hands.

Kate bowed her head, shoulders shaking with the force of her grief. Beside her, James shifted, one broad palm coming to rest on the nape of her neck. The touch was warm and grounding, against the sorrow that threatened to pull her under.

Time lost all meaning in that little room, the seconds bleeding into minutes into hours. Kate talked until her throat ached and her voice was little more than a rasp. She shared memories of happier times, of laughter and love and the kind of bone-deep connection that could never be severed, not even by death. And through it all, James remained a silent guardian against the riptide of despair.

It was the doctor's gentle knock that finally shattered the timeless bubble they'd crafted, the illusion of a world narrowed down to just the three of them. Kate glanced up, blinking gritty eyes as the man in the white coat slipped into the room, a somber figure carrying the weight of impending loss.

"It's time," he said simply, apology and compassion mingling in his gaze.

Kate couldn't speak, couldn't force air past the fist of anguish clenched around her larynx. But she managed a nod, a silent assent to the unthinkable.

The doctor moved to the bank of machines with purposeful steps, hands steady as they began the process of unhooking, unfastening, undoing. Kate watched, numb and distant, as the ventilator wheezed to a stop, as the heart monitor stuttered and slowed.

And then there was only silence, vast and yawning, a chasm with no bottom. Kate stared at her father's face, at the slackness of his features in repose. Waiting for the miracle, for the gasping inhale and fluttering lids of every hospital drama she'd ever seen.

But there was only stillness, only the gray pallor of death creeping across Walter's sunken cheeks.

A sob wrenched itself from Kate's chest, a sound like something tearing, something vital giving way. She folded over her father's body, clutching his limp hand to her cheek as the grief crashed over her in relentless waves.

Distantly, she registered movement, the doctor's murmured condolences as he slipped out, the rustle of James's clothing as he dropped to his knees beside her chair. Then strong arms were enveloping her, pulling her into the shelter of his embrace as she shattered, as the howling void where her heart had been threatened to swallow her whole.

James held her through the worst of it, his own tears soaking her hair as he rocked her like a child. Broken endearments and aching words of comfort fell from his lips, nearly lost beneath the force of her desolation. But somehow, they pierced the haze of agony, tiny pinpricks of light in the endless black.

It could have been minutes or hours later when Kate finally pulled back, her eyes swollen and burning, her throat scraped raw, her sinuses inflamed. James reached out to cradle her face in his palms, thumbs sweeping away the tracks of moisture on her cheeks.

"I've got you," he promised, his voice thick and unsteady. "I'm here, and I swear, I'm not going anywhere."

Kate managed a jerky nod, turning her head to press a kiss to his palm. Inhaling deeply, she forced herself to look back at the bed, at the empty shell that had once housed her father's brilliant spirit.

"Goodbye, Daddy," she whispered, fresh tears spilling hotly down her face. "I love you. I love you, and I...I hope you're at peace."

The words felt hollow, inadequate. But they were all she had left to give.

With a final, shuddering breath, Kate allowed James to pull her to her feet, his arm solid and steadying around her waist. Together, they walked out of that room of sorrow and into the blinding light of a world forever changed.

Kate knew with certainty that her trials were far from over. The shadow figure, the painting, her father's enigmatic warnings...all of it waited for her, a dark tide lapping at the edges of her consciousness.

But for now, she let herself lean into the warmth of James's side, let his strength buoy her through the numbness of shock and grief. There would be time enough for battles to come, for facing down the demons that had stolen her father and now threatened to unravel her very sanity.

For now, Kate simply put one foot in front of the other, each step an act of defiance against the darkness nipping at her heels.

Miles away, in the quiet stillness of Walter's studio, the unfinished painting sat upon the easel, the jagged tear in its center like a wound that refused to heal. As the last of the forced oxygen slowly slipped from Walter's lungs, a strange energy began to gather in the room, a palpable sense of presence that seemed to emanate from the canvas itself.

Slowly, almost imperceptibly at first, the edges of the tear began to widen, the fabric of reality stretching and warping like a funhouse mirror. From the depths of the painting, a dark, shadowy figure began to emerge, its form indistinct and ever-shifting, like smoke given shape by the wind.

As the entity passed through the tear, the canvas shuddered and rippled, as if the very fabric of the painting was being rent asunder by its passage. The room grew cold, the temperature plummeting as if the warmth of life itself was being leeched away by the entity's presence.

In the glow from the streetlights outside, the shadows in the studio seemed to lengthen and deepen, taking on a malevolent cast. The entity, partially manifested, hovered before the painting, its form a writhing mass of darkness shot through with veins of sickly, pulsing red.

For a long moment, it remained motionless, as if gathering its strength. And then, with a sudden, violent motion, it lashed out at the painting, its shadowy tendrils tearing at the canvas like claws.

The painting shuddered under the assault, the image of the faceless Eleanor rippling and distorting as if viewed through a veil of tears. And as the entity continued its relentless attack, the painting began to change, the colors fading and running together like a watercolor left out in the rain.

And in the silence that followed, the studio lay still and empty, the only sign of the entity's passage a faint, lingering chill in the air and a sense of unease that seeped into the very walls of the house itself.

For Kate, unaware of the dark forces gathering in her father's home, the true horror of her ordeal was only just beginning. And as she stepped out into the night, the weight of her grief a heavy burden upon her shoulders, she had no idea of the malevolent presence that awaited her, biding its time until the moment was right to strike.

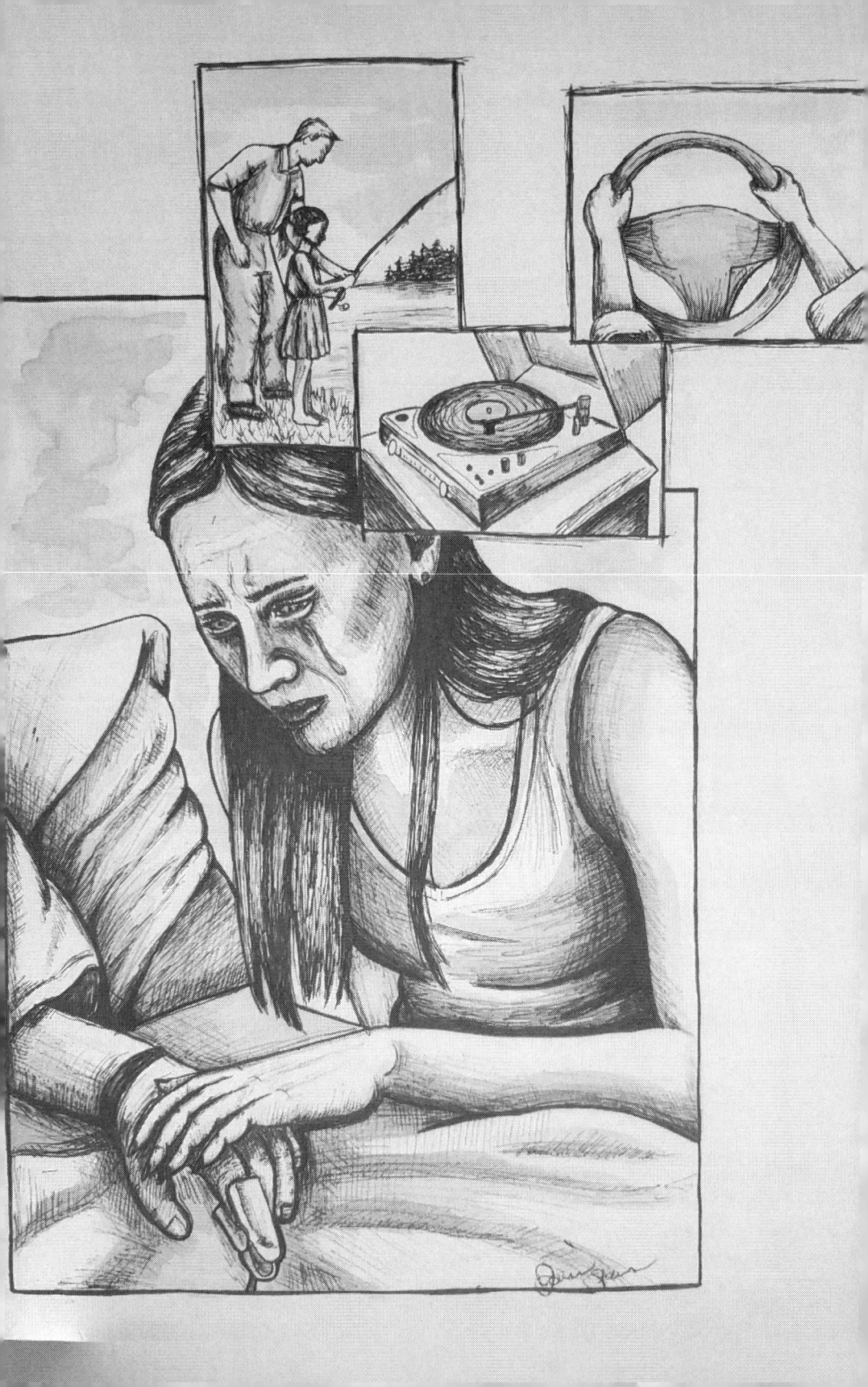

IN DREAMS, A RECKONING

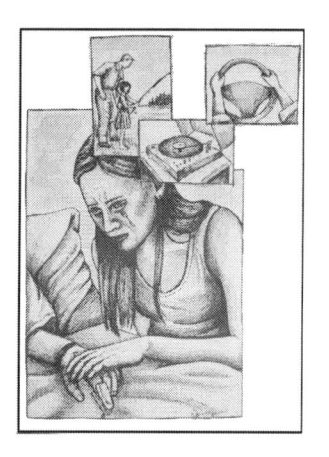

T he drive back to her Walter's house was a blur, rain-slick streets and a gray sky blending together in Kate's memory. Inside, she moved as if in a trance, sinking onto the sofa. James lingered in the doorway, his face etched with uncertainty.

"I can stay," James offered softly, "if you want the company.

Or I can give you some space, let you process..." He trailed off, raking a hand through his disheveled hair.

Kate managed a wan smile, patting the space beside her in silent invitation. "Stay. Please. I...I don't think I can be alone with my thoughts right now."

Relief softened his features as he crossed the room, settling next to her with a sigh. For a long moment, they simply sat in companionable silence, shoulders brushing, the weight of shared sorrow hanging heavy in the air.

Finally, James cleared his throat, turning to catch her gaze. "About earlier," he began, choosing his words with care, "in your dad's studio... I know it might not seem important now, but...I'm here, Kate. Whenever you're ready to talk about...whatever it is you're dealing with. I'm here, and I'll believe you. No matter how crazy it might sound."

Tears pricked the backs of Kate's eyes, her throat tightening at the earnest sincerity in his voice. Impulsively, she reached for his hand, twining her fingers through his and squeezing gently.

"I don't even know where to start," she admitted, hating the tremor in her words. "It's all so surreal, so...impossible. I keep thinking I must be losing my mind, that grief has finally pushed me over the edge into full-blown delusion."

James's thumb swept over her knuckles, his touch achingly tender. "Why don't you start at the beginning?" he suggested. "We've got all the time in the world."

And so, in halting fragments and tearful asides, the story

spilled out of Kate. She told him about that first night in the studio, about the painting that seemed to hold a malevolent life of its own. About the Ouija board and its inexplicable presence in Walter's space. About the dreams that had plagued her since this whole nightmare began. About the recurring crow, swooping in like a bad omen, the warning it heralded.

Through it all, James listened, brow furrowed, eyes dark with concern, but never once interrupting. Never once looking at her like she'd sprouted a second head or started speaking in tongues. When she finally ran out of words, her voice hoarse and her cheeks damp, he simply gathered her into his arms, tucking her head beneath his chin and letting her burrow into the solid strength of his chest.

"I believe you," he murmured into her hair, the words fierce and unflinching. "Every word, Kate. I can't pretend to understand what's happening, but...I believe you."

She shuddered against him, a fragile sound caught somewhere between a sob and a sigh escaping her lips. "I'm so scared, Jimmy. Scared that whatever this...thing...is, it's not done with me. That losing Dad was just the beginning of something so much worse."

His arms tightened around her, as if he could shield her from the malevolent forces at work through sheer determination. "Then we face it together. Whatever comes next, whatever fresh hell is waiting in the wings...you're not alone, Kate. I promise you that."

They clung to each other in the dying light of day, two lost souls adrift in a sea of grief and uncertainty. Kate let herself get lost in the steady thrum of James's heartbeat beneath her ear, in the rise and fall of his chest and the whisper of his breath against her temple. For the first time since this waking nightmare began, she felt the tiniest flicker of something like hope kindling in her chest, though fragile and tenuous, but stubbornly persistent.

As if sensing the direction of her thoughts, James pulled back just far enough to meet her gaze, one calloused palm rising to cup her cheek. "We're going to get through this," he vowed, low and intent. "I don't know how yet, but...we'll find a way. We'll fight this thing with everything we've got, and we'll come out the other side. Together."

Kate managed a wobbly smile, turning her head to press a kiss to his palm. "Together," she echoed, the word a talisman against the darkness.

They stayed like that for a long while, foreheads pressed together, breathing each other's air as the shadows lengthened and the room grew dim. It was only when Kate's stomach gave a traitorous growl that they pulled apart, twin looks of chagrin and weary amusement on their faces.

"Guess I should probably eat something," Kate admitted, scrubbing a hand over her gritty eyes. "Pretty sure my last meal was a stale bagel at the hospital yesterday morning."

James's face softened with a protective urge that ignited a fierce determination within him. Gently tucking a stray strand of hair behind her ear, he suggested, "Why don't you try to rest for a bit? I'll see if I can find something to eat in the kitchen."

A wave of exhaustion washed over Kate, sudden and overwhelming. Her stomach rumbled at the thought of food, but the promise of even a few moments of respite from the relentless churn of her thoughts was too alluring to ignore.

"All right," she agreed, offering a weary smile.

She watched him slip out of the living room and into the kitchen. Then, with limbs gone heavy and eyelids gritty, she let herself sink into the waiting sleep.

It seemed only seconds later that she was jerking awake, heart slamming against her ribs and a scream locked behind her teeth. The room was full dark now, the shadows thick and cloying as they pressed in on her from all sides. Disoriented, Kate fumbled for the lamp on the end table, flinching at the sudden flare of illumination.

A glance at her phone on the coffee table confirmed that she'd been asleep for less than an hour, though it felt like an eternity.

A sudden, sharp cry from kitchen had her rocketing to her feet, adrenaline surging through her veins. "James?" she called, fear pitching her voice high and thready. "Jimmy, are you okay?"

Silence, broken only by the thud of her own pulse in her ears.

Heart in her throat, Kate bolted for the kitchen, James's

name on her lips—only to skid to a halt, horror stealing the breath from her lungs.

There, in the center of the room, stood the shadow figure, towering and terrible, darkness bleeding from its edges like an open wound. And clutched in its skeletal grip, suspended a foot off the ground...was James.

His face was a mask of agony, eyes bulging and mouth gaping as he scrabbled weakly against the monstrous claw wrapped around his throat. The creature seemed to pulse with malevolent glee, its head cocked as it watched its prey struggle and gasp.

"No!" The scream tore from Kate's chest, raw and desperate. She lunged forward, heedless of the danger, every instinct screaming at her to save him, to put herself between James and this nightmare made flesh.

But before she could take more than a step, the shadow figure's head swiveled toward her, the void of its face seeming to crackle with dark amusement. With a flick of its wrist, it sent James hurtling across the room, his body slamming into the refrigerator with a sickening crunch before crumpling to the floor in a heap.

"James!" Kate's feet were moving before conscious thought could catch up, propelling her toward his prone form. But the shadow man was faster, gliding across the space between them with preternatural speed. One elongated limb shot out, wrapping around her waist and yanking her off her feet as if she weighed nothing at all.

The air left her lungs in a rush as she found herself dangling in the creature's grasp, its touch searing her skin even through the barrier of her clothing. Up close, the wrongness of it was overwhelming— the oily sheen of its hide, the noxious stench of decay that rolled off it in putrid waves. Kate gagged, tears streaming down her face as she thrashed and bucked, desperate to break free.

But it was like fighting smoke, like grappling with a thing made of nightmare and shadow. The harder she struggled, the tighter its grip became, until spots were dancing before her eyes and her lungs were screaming for air.

Through the haze of pain and terror, she heard James groan weakly, saw him struggling to push himself upright on trembling arms. The shadow man's head turned toward the sound, a grotesque approximation of a smile splitting the seam of its mouth.

"No," Kate gasped, the word thin and thready. "No, please...leave him alone. It's me you want, right? Just...just take me and let him go."

The thing's head swiveled back toward her, considering. For a breathless moment, Kate was sure it would refuse, that it would toss her aside and finish James off right before her eyes, just for the savage joy of it.

But then, to her shock, it opened its hand, letting her crumple to the floor in a graceless heap. She lay there, chest heaving as she sucked in desperate lungfuls of air, watching through streaming eyes as the creature loomed over her.

"Go on then," she spat, pushing herself shakily to her hands and knees. "Take me, you bastard. But leave him out of it. This is between you and me."

The shadow man's laugh was a physical thing, a skittering, chitinous sound that crawled over her skin like a thousand scuttling insects. It bent at the waist, skeletal fingers outstretched, reaching for her with an almost lover-like tenderness that turned her stomach.

Kate closed her eyes, bracing for the feel of that unholy touch, for the pain and the cold and the sinking certainty of her own doom. But it never came.

Instead, there was a blinding flash of light, a searing wash of heat that sent her reeling back with a cry. The shadow figure shrieked—an unearthly, soul-rending sound—and reared away from her, its form contorting and rippling like a thing in agony.

Squinting against the glare, Kate blinked tears from her lashes, struggling to make sense of what she was seeing. There, standing in the doorway with a wild look in his eyes...was James. In his hand he held a crucifix, the one Eleanor had hung on the wall beside the refrigerator, where the landline phone once was.

His lips moved soundlessly, the words lost beneath the shadow man's piercing wails. But as Kate watched in shock, she saw the creature begin to falter, its limbs shriveling and blackening like paper thrust into a flame. It staggered, clawing at its own chest as if trying to rip the light from its body, but to no avail.

With a final, guttural scream, the shadow man burst apart—shards of darkness scattering like ash on the wind until nothing remained but an oily smear on the hardwood and the fading echo of its dying howl.

For a moment, the only sound was their ragged breathing, the desperate thunder of Kate's heart in her ears. Then James was dropping to his knees beside her—

"Kate," James croaked, shaking her roughly, startling her awake. "Oh God, Kate, are you okay?"

She shook her head mutely, still too stunned to speak. Gingerly, she pushed herself upright. They were both on the sofa where she'd fallen asleep.

"I'm okay," she managed finally, the words thin and reedy. "I'm...Jesus, Jimmy, what the hell just happened?"

He barked a nervous laugh, the sound edged with hysteria. "I was going to ask you that question. You were having a nightmare. I've been trying to wake you for five minutes. You were screaming and thrashing around and I couldn't wake you."

The reality of their situation crashed over Kate like a wave, stealing the breath from her lungs. But beneath the fear...there was something else. Something bright and fierce, kindling to life in her chest like an ember. Something that felt strangely, impossibly, like hope.

Kate leaned forward until her forehead rested against his,

their breath mingling in the scant space between them. "I'm sorry."

"Don't be sorry. None of this is your fault," he said, and kissed her. Her hands were at his face now, pulling his lips tighter against hers, the ball of her thumb tracing the scar across his stubbled cheek.

TE MYSTERIOUS MOURNER

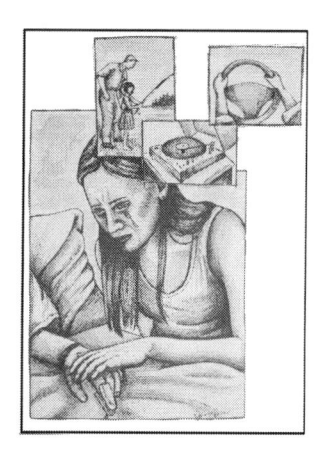

The morning was warm, the sunlight filtering through the leafy canopy of the cemetery's ancient trees in dappled puddles of gold. Kate stood motionless, her eyes fixed on the casket as it was slowly lowered into the cold earth. A slight breeze picked up, lifting strands of her dark hair and sending them dancing across her cheeks. She barely noticed, too focused on keeping her breathing steady, on holding herself together. It wasn't right that the world could be so lovely, the sky so vivid a blue, when everything inside her was turning to ashes and dust.

Guilt, heavy as a stone, sat like a weight in her chest. It pressed against her ribs, making each breath an effort, threatening to bring her to her knees right there in the cemetery grass. All the things she'd left unsaid to her father, the moments she'd let slip away, came crashing back in painful clarity. Each memory an accusation, an unspoken apology that would forever go unheard by the one person who needed it most.

Kate clenched her jaw, fighting against the emotion rising in her throat. She imagined that insurmountable weight crushing her, pushing her down into the dirt to rest beside the coffin. Maybe that was what she deserved. A fitting punishment for her failures. Her eyes burned but no tears came. She wondered if she'd ever feel anything again, besides this aching, hollow emptiness.

Beside her, James shifted slightly, the sleeve of his suit jacket brushing her arm, a reminder that she wasn't alone, that he was there, solid and steady. Kate wanted to reach for him, to lace her fingers through his and hold on for dear life. But she couldn't make her hands work, couldn't tear her eyes away from the rectangle of darkness that had swallowed her father whole.

The priest was speaking, the rise and fall of his voice a

distantly familiar cadence. Kate heard the words, but they slid over her like oil on water, leaving no impression. Ashes to ashes. Dust to dust. The body in the casket was her father, but not. Everything that had made him Walter—his brilliant mind, his wry humor, the way he'd looked at her over his reading glasses, one bushy brow lifted, his strong hands working tools as he bent over the engine of the Mustang—was gone, as lost to her as her mother

She was an orphan now. The last of her small, splintered family. The realization crashed over her like a wave, sudden and overwhelming, and Kate had to lock her knees to keep from swaying. She'd thought she was ready for this, that she'd cried herself out, wrung her grief into every corner of Walter's empty house. But standing here, watching her father vanish into the hungry earth...it was too much.

Too final.

The service passed in a haze of murmured condolences. Kate moved through it mechanically, the priest's words washing over her, the rituals as familiar and distant as a childhood lullaby. Sympathy from strangers, friends, and colleagues blurred together until the faces were just smears of color, the voices a droning hum. None of it seemed real—not the gleaming casket, not the mound of fresh earth waiting to swallow it, not the terrible finality of her father's name carved into unyielding granite.

It was as the mourners began to drift toward the grave that Kate saw her. A lone figure standing apart from the others, a slash of black against the green rolling hill and grave markers. She was young, too young to be one of Walter's contemporaries, with short dark hair and eyes hidden behind even darker framed glasses. But she stared at the casket with an intensity that seared, her gaze unwavering even as the priest droned on.

Something about her troubled Kate, a splinter of unease beneath her numbness. She found herself staring, trying to place the woman, to understand her presence here, her relationship to Walter.

For a moment, their gazes locked across the expanse of manicured grass and dulled headstones. The woman's head tilted, something knowing in the gesture, and then the priest invited the mourners forward for the final goodbye.

Kate jerked back to herself, the world rushing in to fill the strange suspended second. Beside her, James shifted. "All right?"

Kate managed a tiny nod. Together, they stepped up to the yawning mouth of the grave. Damp earth, cold and heavy in her palm. It sifted through her fingers and pattered against the glossy wood, each muffled thump an unvoiced apology, an unspoken plea for absolution. Her throat closed around the words she hadn't said, the questions forever left unanswered.

When it was over, when the last prayer had been murmured and the mourners began to scatter, Kate turned back, seeking out the mysterious woman with a sudden, desperate urgency. But she was gone, vanished into the sea of black-clad figures as if she'd never been.

"James," Kate whispered, her voice cracking on his name. "Did you see her? The woman in the back, with the short dark hair and glasses. I didn't recognize her, but the way she was staring at the casket...She knew Walter. I'm sure of it."

"I didn't notice... But then, I wasn't really looking. Could she have been here for someone else?" James frowned, his gaze sweeping across the thinning crowd. "For another service maybe?"

Kate shook her head, cold certainty settling like a stone in her stomach. "No, it was more than that. The way she looked at me, at the casket...I can't explain it, but I just know she was here for him. That she *knew* him."

James's brow furrowed, but his hand tightened around hers, anchoring her. "Okay. I mean, we can... We'll figure it out, Kate. But for now, let's just get through the rest of today. One thing at a time, yeah?"

"Yeah." The word was little more than a breath. "One thing at a time."

But even as James led her toward the waiting car, Kate couldn't stop thinking about the unknown woman. Her mind kept returning to the question of who she was and why she was there, examining it from every angle with an almost obsessive focus. Something about the woman's presence seemed important, significant.

Letting out a shuddering breath, Kate allowed him to lead

her toward the waiting line of cars, to the somber procession that would take them to the small reception hall James had rented for the post-funeral gathering. She moved through the rituals in a daze, accepting condolences and murmured platitudes with a flat, fixed smile, searching for the woman while picking at the food that tasted like ash on her tongue.

All the while, her mind churned with thoughts of the mysterious mourner, with the gnawing certainty that her presence was more than mere coincidence. It was a puzzle piece that didn't fit, a discordant note in the symphony of her sorrow, and Kate couldn't shake the feeling that it somehow tied back to the nightmares that had haunted her and whatever happened to Walter in the study.

By the time the last straggling guest had departed with a final squeeze of her hand and a whispered "sorry for your loss," Kate was vibrating out of her skin, exhaustion and grief and the constant, low-level thrum of wrongness coalescing into a jittery sort of mania. James, bless him, seemed to sense her unraveling, gently shepherded her out to the car and bundled her into the passenger seat with a soft touch and a murmured assurance.

The drive back to Walter's house passed in merciful quiet, the silence broken only by the hum of the engine and the occasional sniffle from Kate as she struggled to maintain her composure. When James pulled into the driveway and killed the ignition, she allowed herself a single, shuddering exhale, the iron bands around her chest loosening fractionally.

"I think... I think I need a minute," she managed, her voice wavering like a warped record. "To change my clothes, to breathe, to just...process."

James's smile was soft and achingly understanding. "Of course. Take all the time you need. I'll go put on some coffee, maybe throw together a quick bite to eat. I don't know about you, but funeral sandwiches always taste like cardboard to me."

A strangled little laugh hiccuped out of her, there and gone. "Thanks, Jimmy," she whispered, leaning across the center console to press a swift, impulsive kiss to his stubbled cheek. "For...god, for everything. I couldn't have made it through today without you."

He caught her hand as she pulled back, cradling it between his broad palms like something precious and fragile. "You don't ever have to thank me, Kate. Not for this. You...you're not alone, okay? Whatever you need, whenever you need it...I'm here. I'm right here, and I'm not going anywhere."

Blinking back the sudden sting of tears, Kate gave him a wobbly nod and slipped out of the car, the soles of her sensible black heels clacking against the sun-warmed concrete of the driveway. She made her way into the house on autopilot, her legs carrying her up the stairs and into the bathroom as if of their own volition.

It was only when the door snicked shut behind her, when the muffled sounds of James puttering around the kitchen faded into white noise, that she allowed herself to shatter. Perched on the closed lid of the toilet, arms wrapped around her middle as if to physically hold herself together, Kate let the tears come, great, silent, racking sobs that felt ripped from some raw, primal place deep in her chest.

She cried for her father, for the wasted years and the words left unsaid. She cried for her mother, for the void Eleanor's death had left in their small family, a festering wound that time had scabbed over but never truly healed. And she cried for herself, motherless, fatherless, alone in the world but for the steadfast man moving around in the kitchen below, the boy she'd left behind and the man who'd crashed back into her life with the force of a revelation.

Slowly, like a tide going out, the tears ebbed, leaving her hollowed out and aching, a shipwreck washed up on unfamiliar shores. With trembling hands, Kate stripped out of her solemn black dress and sheer stockings, shrugging into the comfort of worn sweatpants and an oversized t-shirt. The face that stared back at her from the mirror was blotchy and ravaged, eyes swollen and nose red from crying, but there was a curious lightness to it too, as if some small part of the terrible burden she'd been carrying had been washed away in the flood of her grief.

Splashing some tepid water on her cheeks, Kate drew in a fortifying breath and made her way downstairs, the rich, earthy scent of ground coffee beans helping to settle her jangled nerves. She found James in the kitchen, shirtsleeves rolled up and hair disheveled, fiddling with the ancient coffee maker with a look of intense concentration on his handsome face.

He glanced up as she padded in on bare feet, his eyes going soft and warm in a way that made her stomach swoop. "Hey. Feeling any better?"

"A bit," she admitted, drifting closer and hopping up to perch on the edge of the counter. "It's all still a bit surreal, you know? Like...like I'm sleepwalking, or trapped in a nightmare I can't quite wake up from."

James made a low, sympathetic noise as he pushed the coffee grinder aside and moved to stand between her dangling legs. His hands came up to frame her face, thumbs sweeping gently over the delicate skin beneath her eyes.

"I can't even imagine what you must be feeling right now," he murmured, searching her gaze with an intensity that stole her breath. "I wish...Christ, Kate, I wish I could take even a fraction of this pain away from you. I hate seeing you hurting like this."

"You are," she whispered, turning her head to press a kiss to his palm. "Taking it away, I mean. Just by being here, by being you."

She swallowed hard, suddenly overwhelmed by the sheer depth of emotion shining in his eyes, by the magnitude of all the things still left unspoken between them. But before she could find the words, before she could take that flying leap into the uncharted territory of her own heart...the shrill peal of the doorbell shattered the fragile intimacy of the moment.

They both started, twin looks of confusion passing over their features. Kate hopped down from the counter, brow furrowed as she made her way to the front door with James trailing behind. She couldn't imagine who would be dropping by unannounced, especially so soon after the funeral.

But when she pulled open the door and found herself staring at the young bespectacled woman from the cemetery, the mysterious mourner whose presence had needled at Kate like a persistent splinter, she was silently shocked.

"Hi," the woman said, her voice a low, soothing contralto. "I'm sorry to intrude, especially on a day like today. You don't know me, but...I was an acquaintance of your Walter's. My name is Tiqua Lovett."

Nightmare Manifestation

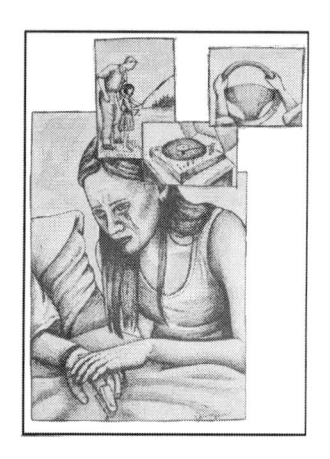

Kate gaped at her, shock and a strange, instinctive recognition battling for dominance in her chest. Behind her, she felt James go still, sensing the sudden coil of tension in his frame as he too absorbed the unexpected visitor.

"I'm sorry," Kate managed, shaking her head as if to clear it. "You said your name was Tiqua? And you knew my father?"

Tiqua inclined her head, sympathy softening her striking features. "I did. And I know you must have questions. It's...well, it's a bit of a long story. May I come in?"

Kate hesitated, her instinct battling with her desperate need for answers. Yet, there was something about Tiqua—a quiet gravity, an aura of wisdom that belied her youthful face—that compelled Kate to step back and gesture for her to enter.

As she closed the door, Kate caught James's eye, saw the flicker of concern and cautious curiosity in his gaze. He stepped forward, offering Tiqua his hand and a slightly strained smile.

"James Nowak," he introduced himself. "I'm a friend of Kate's. And of Walter's."

Tiqua clasped his hand briefly, her own smile small but genuine. "A pleasure. I only wish we were meeting under better circumstances."

An awkward beat passed with the weight of their shared loss hanging heavy in the air. Then Kate cleared her throat and ushered them all into the living room with a forced semblance of normality.

"Please, have a seat," Kate offered, perching on the edge of the sofa and trying to ignore the way her pulse jumped and fluttered in her throat. "Can I get you anything? Water? Coffee?"

THE DEVIL'S DOORWAY

"Coffee is good," Tiqua said, sitting in Walter's chair that seemed to swallow up her small frame.

"I'll take care of it," James said, brushing a reassuring hand over Kate's shoulder. "You two...talk."

And then he was gone, disappearing into the kitchen with a final backward glance, leaving Kate alone with the enigmatic woman who had known her father in ways she did not yet understand.

"So," Kate began, twisting her fingers together in her lap, a nervous habit she was unaware of. "How is it you know my father?"

Tiqua exhaled softly, something pained and distant in her eyes. "Walter reached out to me about three months ago. He found my website and contacted me with questions about...about connecting with a loved one who had passed on."

Kate felt her brow furrow, a hot little knot of confusion tightening behind her breastbone.

Seeing the confused look on Kate's face, Tiqua offered a gentle smile and clarified, "I am a medium. I communicate with the spirits of those who have passed on. My work often involves Tarot readings, where I use the cards to gain insight and guidance. But I also conduct séances on occasion. These are more involved rituals where I attempt to directly connect with and channel spirits, allowing them to communicate with the living through me."

"Eleanor," Kate said, the name barely a whisper. "My mother. He wanted to reach out to her, didn't he?"

"Yes." Tiqua's voice was gentle, suffused with a sorrow that made Kate's teeth ache. "He was...when we first spoke, it was clear that he was struggling. Drowning in his grief. I got the sense that he'd never really processed your mother's loss, not fully anyway. That some part of him was still clinging to the hope of a reunion, even after all this time. He had something he felt he needed to say to her and he couldn't be free of his guilt until he had."

Kate's throat closed, tears stinging the backs of her eyes. It hurt, imagining her strong, steady father brought so low by the weight of his mourning. The idea of him reaching out to this stranger in the dark, grasping for any chance to communicate with her mother again, if only for a moment, was gut-wrenching.

She was grateful for the distraction of James's return, for the clinking of the coffee tray as he set it on the table and the rich, earthy scent of freshly brewed beans. The ritual of pouring and preparing their cups gave Kate a moment to collect herself, to swallow past the jagged lump of unshed tears lodged in her throat.

When she'd regained some modicum of control, she met Tiqua's gaze head-on, steeling herself for the rest of the story. "So you...what? Performed a reading for him? Tried to contact my mother?"

Tiqua cradled her mug between slim hands, seeming to

THE DEVIL'S DOORWAY

choose her next words with care. "We first met at my shop and did a few sessions, yes. With very limited success. I could sense Eleanor's presence around us, but the connection was always tenuous, flickering. Like trying to catch smoke in your bare hands."

She paused, taking a fortifying sip of coffee before continuing. "Walter grew increasingly frustrated and more desperate after each session. He became convinced that if we attempted contact in a place that held strong memories, had a powerful emotional resonance for the deceased...it might strengthen the link. Bridge the gap between worlds more fully."

A shiver walked its way down Kate's spine, a cold finger of foreboding trailing ice in its wake. "He asked you to come here," she said, the words leaden on her tongue. "To the house, didn't he?"

"He did." Tiqua's gaze cut away, fixing on some distant point beyond Kate's shoulder.

The hairs on the back of Kate's neck prickled, a slow, cold dread unfurling in her gut. Beside her, James had gone preternaturally still, his face gave away nothing of what he was feeling or thinking.

"What happened?" Kate asked, fighting to keep her voice steady. "During that session?"

Tiqua's eyes met hers, dark and haunted. "Walter... he was extremely frustrated with my methods, feeling they weren't yielding the connection he desperately sought. When I showed up with my Tarots, he surprised me—he had divination tool, a spirit board he believed might serve as a stronger conduit, providing a more direct line of communication."

"The Ouija board," Kate said.

Tiqua nodded, her fingers wrapped firmly around the mug.

"So it wasn't yours, the Ouija?"

Tiqua shook her head. "No, I don't use them in my practice. It was here already, in his studio."

"Do you know where he got it?"

"I don't. He didn't say."

Kate chewed at her bottom lip a moment, then asked, "Can I ask...why the aversion to the Ouija?"

"Ouija boards...they have a reputation for a reason. They are powerful, yes, but also unpredictable and difficult to control. I prefer to work with my cards and crystals, tools that allow me to maintain a degree of autonomy, of authority over the connection."

Her jaw tightened, a muscle twitching beneath her skin. "But Walter...he was desperate. Almost frantic in his need to try anything, exhaust every possibility. I could see the depth of his pain, how desperately he wanted—*needed*—to believe this would be the answer. And so—against my better judgment—I gave in, agreed to use the board that night."

Kate's stomach churned, a greasy sort of nausea rising in the back of her throat. She thought of the sickly, oily feel of the shadow man in her nightmare, of the malevolent weight of the presence that had dogged her steps and haunted her dreams since the moment she'd set foot back in this house.

Kate looked directly at Tiqua, her gaze intense and questioning. "It worked, didn't it?" she asked, her voice emerging rough and strained. "You made contact with...someone?"

Tiqua closed her eyes and hunched forward, her shoulders tense and rigid. She remained quiet for a time, her expression pained and distressed. When she finally spoke, her words were soft and faint, almost inaudible in the room's stillness. "Yes. But not...not with Eleanor."

The question lingered, its weight palpable in the space separating them. Kate felt her insides lurch and a wave of faintness washed over her. She fought to push down the rapidly growing lump in her throat, managing to choke out, "Then who?"

Tiqua trembled, her entire frame shaking in a way that caused Kate's arm hair to rise. Hesitantly at first, then with building momentum, Tiqua started talking. The words spilled forth from her mouth, each one falling heavily into the space between them, gradually picking up speed and volume like a gathering rockslide.

"It all happened so fast," Tiqua said quietly, her voice trembling slightly as she stared off into the distance, eyes unfocused and clouded by the memory of fear. "The planchette began moving without any of us touching it. Suddenly, there was this sensation of something else in the room. A presence that was oppressive, foreboding, and filled with what felt like hatred and cruel intent. It seemed as if something terrible had broken free from somewhere far away and somehow malevolent, and forced its way into the studio to join us. Something awful and ravenous..."

Kate's nails bit into her palms, her pulse a deafening drumbeat in her ears. In her mind's eye, she saw again the grotesque figure from her dream, the towering, emaciated form, the grasping claws, the shadows that clung to it like a noxious shroud.

"It assaulted me," she managed to say, struggling to get the words out through the constriction in her throat. "The strength behind it was beyond anything I'd previously encountered. It...it picked me up completely, hurling me from one side of the room to the other as though I was weightless. When it threw me to the ground, the impact was so severe I nearly lost consciousness."

Her fingers moved tentatively toward her shoulder, gently exploring the remembered pain as her mind revisited the past. "Walter was intensely focused, absolutely certain that Eleanor was present... I pleaded with him repeatedly to break the link, but he refused to heed my words, wouldn't see the truth."

Kate felt a wave of nausea and the tell-tale sting of unshed tears. James placed his palm against her lower back, the warmth and solidity of his touch offering a measure of comfort amid the disturbing details being shared.

"I panicked," she confessed, her face drawn with a deep, private pain that etched into every line of her face. "I should have stayed, should have tried to help him. But I was...I was so *terrified*. It was like staring into the face of pure evil, like feeling my very soul shrivel in the presence of something so utterly unholy. I...I ran. I abandoned him there, alone with that...that *evil...and I ran.*"

"It wasn't your fault," Kate managed, fighting down the hot swell of nausea. "You couldn't have known. Couldn't have predicted..." She trailed off, unable to give voice to the magnitude of the horror Tiqua described.

The other woman, however, disagreed, her dark eyes reflecting a determined resoluteness. "No, Kate, this is my responsibility. I made a mistake in agreeing to use that Ouija board, regardless of Walter's distress and persuasion. I was aware of the potential consequences, I understood the risks..." Her voice faded. Meeting Kate's gaze, her eyes glistened with unshed tears. "I called the police, told them I heard noises coming from the house. I just couldn't bring myself to go back...in here...up there...but I wanted to get help."

"So, you're the one who called the police," Kate said, the question of who had called the authorities now settled. A new thought struck her, and she inhaled sharply. "Did...did that thing...cause my father's stroke?"

Tiqua hesitated before responding. "It's hard to say for certain. Tangible manifestations of this nature are quite uncommon..." Her voice faded as she focused more intently on Kate, staring at her with a penetrating look that left Kate feeling breathless and unsettled.

"Kate, I need you to understand something," she said, her voice low and serious. "The entity we communicated with—it's still here. I can feel it now. A force of corruption and hunger lurking just beyond the veil. Growing stronger, more solid, with each passing day.

"Using a Ouija board is like opening a passageway, a portal between worlds we were never meant to touch. And if opened carelessly, without proper safeguards and precautions...it's impossible to predict what entities or forces might cross over. There's a risk that something could latch onto our reality, establishing a presence in this world that we may not be equipped to handle or control."

Kate felt an uneasy sensation wash over her as she involuntarily glanced up at the ceiling, to the invisible weight of the studio pressing down from above. The room where it had all begun and where it was all beginning again, the painted door swinging wide to beckon in the shadows.

James's voice cut through the momentary silence, startling Kate. "You should tell her, Kate." His tone was gentle but urgent, a quiet demand.

Until now, he'd been a silent presence at her side, listening to Tiqua talk of Tarot and Ouija and connecting with spirits, of doorways to between worlds that should never have been opened. His face had given nothing away, but Kate felt the tension radiating off him, saw the way his jaw clenched and his eyes narrowed. He was struggling to believe, to reconcile the supernatural with the natural.

She'd expected him to scoff, to dismiss it all as nonsense and fantasy. God knew, she wanted to. But James wasn't laughing. He wasn't dismissing or denying. He was looking at her, his gaze steady and unwavering, and Kate realized with a jolt that he did believe. Believed in communing with the dead, in unholy things crossing over from some other, darker place. Believed...because she did, because of what she'd experienced.

The knowledge hit her like a punch to the gut, stealing her breath. After everything she'd told him, everything she'd shared...he was still here. Still by her side, steady as a heartbeat. Trusting in her, even when what she was saying sounded like the ravings of a madwoman.

Something cracked open in Kate's chest, a fissure of warmth in the icy wasteland of her grief. She swallowed hard around the sudden lump in her throat, blinking back the sting of tears.

"James..."

He reached out, clasped her hand in his. His palm was warm, calloused, achingly familiar. "It's okay, Kate. She needs to know. So she can help."

Kate gripped his hand tightly, clinging to him as if he were the only stable presence in an unstable situation. Taking a deep breath, she looked directly at Tiqua, who waited patiently. Slowly and hesitantly, she started to recount her experiences, beginning with the unsettling dream in which Walter's indistinct voice, barely audible amid the buzzing of insects, urged her to shut the door. She then described receiving the call from the hospital and encountering the odd crow in the parking garage, which had been perched on the car's hood and later appeared on the hospital window ledge, pecking insistently at the glass. The same crow, she revealed, had also manifested on the back of the chair where Tiqua was currently sitting, appearing and disappearing abruptly, its strange voice insisting, "Close." Kate went on to detail discovering the Ouija board, noticing the charred floorboards, and perceiving the shadowy figure standing behind the woman in the painting, its taloned hand placed on her shoulder, and how the woman's blank face had seemingly come to life, contorting into a terrifying and repulsive visage.

Tiqua listened intently as Kate spoke, her brow furrowing, her lips pursed in concentration. One hand was cupped over her mouth, as if to physically hold back the questions and fears that threatened to spill out.

When Kate finally fell silent. She felt flayed open, raw and exposed beneath the bright, assessing gaze of the other woman.

"I don't know what to do, Tiqua," she said, her voice emerged thin and uncertain, nearly swallowed by the vast depth of her own fear. "How can I put an end to this?" Her words hung in the air, a fragile plea for guidance in the face of an overwhelming situation.

"How do *we* put an end to this?" James corrected, his voice firm, unyielding. He squeezed her hand, a silent promise. Not alone. Never alone.

Tiqua remained silent for a while, her gaze unfocused as if she were deep in thought. When she finally spoke, her voice was measured and even, her words carefully chosen and delivered with a sense of certainty and finality that suggested she had given the matter serious consideration and arrived at a conclusion that seemed, to her, inescapable.

"I need to see it. The painting. The place where you saw the entity manifest," she said, her eyes meeting Kate's with a sharp, focused intensity. "I know it's awful, Kate. I can't imagine the horror you must have felt. But if I'm to have any hope of helping you fight this thing...I need to understand exactly what we're facing."

Kate's body trembled involuntarily as she contemplated entering the room once more. A wave of nausea swept over her, the bitter taste of fear rising in her mouth. Yet, underneath the layers of anxiety and apprehension, a small but resilient flame began to burn. It was a glimmer of resolve, of purpose forged through the depths of grief and suffering. This tiny ember of courage, born from the ashes of her past experiences, now kindled within her, urging her forward despite the overwhelming desire to turn away.

Walter was gone, devoured by the darkness he'd unwittingly invited in. Yet Kate remained, still intact regardless of all that had occurred. She was fiercely determined not to allow this repugnant, insidious force to claim even a shred more from her or those dear to her.

"All right," Kate said, her voice unwavering and filled with a resolve that surprised even herself. She looked directly at Tiqua, her eyes locked on the other woman's, her determination unwavering. "All right. I'm ready. Let's go."

Kate took a steadying breath and ascended the staircase, making her way to the studio. This space had been the origin point, the genesis of everything that followed and where—one way or another—it would finally end.

As she stepped inside, the odor assaulted her senses before anything else—an overwhelming combination of decay and sulfur that triggered her gag reflex. Next to her, James let out a soft, distressed sound as he reached for her hand, gripping it firmly. Tiqua appeared visibly unsettled, her complexion pallid in the low light.

"Jesus, where is that smell coming from?" James asked, lifting his arm to cover his nose and mouth.

But Kate ignored him, her attention inexorably drawn to the painting. The unsettling image exerted an almost hypnotic pull that she felt powerless to oppose. In the low light, the painting appeared to throb with a strange energy. The garish slash through the canvas gaped before her, simultaneously beckoning and threatening, as if it were a portal to something twisted and harmful.

"God," Tiqua breathed as she approached the easel with measured steps. "The darkness...it's unusually intense in this spot, so concentrated."

James trailed after the women into the room, feeling disconnected from his surroundings, as if sleepwalking. He came to a halt beside Tiqua and gazed at the painting, an almost tangible sensation of unease crawling across his skin, like countless invisible insects.

Tiqua's throat constricted as she gulped, her expression shifting to one of grim acceptance. "I have to examine it more thoroughly, to observe what you did." Her eyes darted to the desk, focusing on the ornate wooden planchette resting on the surface of the Ouija board. "May I...?"

Kate managed a nod in response, her throat constricted with emotion. She observed as Tiqua extended her hand, grasping the planchette with her delicate fingers. Tiqua raised the small wooden piece, bringing it up to her face for a closer examination.

What happened next seemed to unfold in slow motion, like a lucid dream that Kate was powerless to escape. Tiqua lifted the planchette, its intricate lens making contact with her glasses with a gentle tap. She drew in a swift, stunned breath as the blood rapidly receded from her face, giving the impression of a sped-up video capturing a wilting bloom. A violent shudder racked her body, causing her grip on the planchette to slacken and nearly sending it tumbling from her abruptly weakened grasp.

Her voice, now thin and strained from fear, rose in pitch as she spoke: "Oh God. Oh sweet merciful God—"

The Ouija board suddenly vibrated against the table, and the planchette jerked out of Tiqua's fingers as though pulled by an unseen force. It clattered to the ground and then, moving as if possessed of its own volition, climbed up the desk leg. The planchette careened erratically back and forth across the desktop, its movements seemingly imbued with an uncanny intentionality, before finally coming to rest in the middle of the board. Slowly, it settled over the word "GOOD-BYE," as though delivering a final, ominous message.

And then, with a sound like tearing silk, the fissure in the painting expanded, creating a rift that seemed to penetrate the underlying structure of existence itself, unleashing a darkness too terrible to name. The entity that began to claw its way out of the breach was a nightmare made flesh, all gaunt, spindly appendages, scrabbling talons, and an undulating, tenebrous form that pulsed like a malignant tumor.

Kate screamed, the sound ripped from her throat involuntarily. Dimly, she registered Tiqua stumbling backward and falling, limbs askew like a marionette with her strings cut. Heard James shouting her name, his voice high and ragged with panic. But it was all distant, muffled, meaningless against the thundering of her pulse in her ears. The roar of the hellish void as it rushed up to swallow her whole.

And then, like a switch being flipped, everything stopped. It all just...ceased, blinking out of existence as if it had never been, leaving Kate standing in the middle of the studio, chest heaving and eyes wild, staring at the painting that sat placid and unchanged on its easel.

SHATTERING CIRCLE

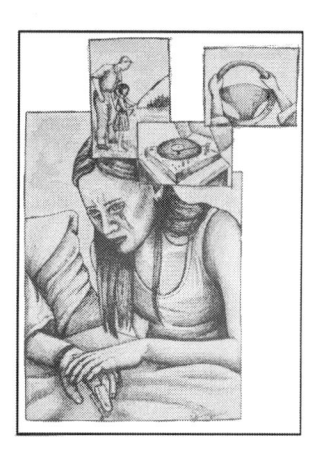

Kate's fingers dug into James's hand, her grip tight and unyielding. James's eyes locked with Tiqua's, his face a mirror of the terror that had taken root within him.

"What...what the fuck was that?" he asked, his voice unsteady and halting. The words felt heavy and awkward as he spoke, inadequate to express the intense fear that gripped him.

Tiqua's complexion had paled, and her brown eyes held a grim understanding. She inhaled slowly, the breath unsteady as she took a moment to collect herself. It was clear she needed to gather her resolve before putting her thoughts into words.

"It's a demon," she whispered, her voice barely audible yet heavy with the grim truth of her words. "An ancient, malevolent entity that feasts on human suffering, gorging itself on despair and anguish."

She paused, letting the gravity of her words sink in. Kate felt a shudder ripple through her, an icy finger trailing down her spine. Beside her, James had gone preternaturally still, tension radiating from him like heat from a furnace.

"Such creatures are drawn to unresolved grief, to the kind of soul-deep pain that leaves a person vulnerable, hollowed out. Walter's loss, his desperation to reconnect with Eleanor...it must have been like a beacon, an irresistible lure to the it."

James's hand tightened around hers, his palm clammy. "How do we stop it?" he asked, voice rough with barely suppressed fear. "There has to be a way to get rid of it, to make it leave."

Tiqua looked at them both, her expression a mix of determination and dread. "Banishing a demon this powerful is no small feat, maybe not even possible. It will require every ounce of skill and strength I possess."

She gestured to the Ouija board that still thrummed with a dark, oily energy, a pulsating malevolence that made Kate's skin crawl.

"This, the board and the painting...they're linked," Tiqua murmured, the realization curdling in her gut like sour milk. "Two halves of a whole. A gateway that's allowing this entity to manifest in our reality."

James shifted beside Kate, his fingers tightening around hers, seeking and offering reassurance in equal measure. "But it's not...it hasn't fully crossed over?" he asked, his voice tinged with a mix of hope and dread.

Tiqua shook her head, the movement slow and deliberate. "Not yet. It's straddling the threshold between planes right now, not quite fully corporeal. But it's gaining strength, siphoning energy from the echoes of Walter's pain, from our fear."

She turned back to Kate and James, her gaze heavy with dark promise. "To manifest completely, to assume its true form...it needs to consume living souls. Starting with those who called it up...and anyone else it can sink its claws into."

Kate's breath hitched, her voice barely a whisper as a chill slithered down her spine. "You," she said, the realization dawning with horrific clarity. "It's coming for you."

"Us," James said flatly, voicing the horrifying truth that hung unspoken between them. "It's coming for all of *us*."

Tiqua nodded, an apology and resignation etched into the lines of her face. "I will do everything in my power to prevent that," she vowed. "But I need your help. Both of you."

Kate stepped forward, jaw clenched against the tide of fear threatening to choke her. "What do you need us to do?"

Crossing to where she'd dropped her bag in the chaos, Tiqua rummaged inside, producing a worn velvet pouch. "I can perform a ritual, use the cards to channel my abilities and try to sever its connection, to seal the breach. But I'll need you to anchor me, to lend your strength and your connection to Walter.

"If we can't exorcise it, we have to close the doorway. Sever the link between worlds and trap this thing back on its own side before it crosses over."

With deft, purposeful movements, she began to lay out the cards in a complex, spiraling pattern on the scuffed hardwood, the Ouija board a malignant blot at its center. "Your presence, your emotional resonance, will help direct the energy, keep it focused where it needs to go."

Kate watched, half-terrified and half-mesmerized, as the web of cards took shape, a feeling of power thrumming in the air like a plucked harp string. Beside her, James shifted uneasily, his free hand flexing at his side.

"Is it...will it be enough?" he asked, doubt and desperate hope warring in his voice.

Tiqua placed the final card and looked up, something

ancient and unfathomable in her dark eyes. "It has to be," she said simply. "Because if it isn't..."

She let the sentence hang, the unspoken implications ringing loud in the suffocating stillness of the room. Kate shuddered, a sick coldness unfurling in the pit of her stomach.

Drawing in a deep, steadying breath, Tiqua positioned herself cross-legged before the array, the Ouija board thrumming with energy mere inches from her knees. "I need you both to stay close," she instructed, her voice low and intent. "But whatever happens, do not break the circle. Any disruption could be...catastrophic."

Kate and James exchanged a loaded glance, fear and resolve passing between them in a moment of wordless communication. As one, they moved to flank Tiqua, close enough to feel the heat of each other's bodies, the whisper of each unsteady breath.

"It will not go quietly," Tiqua said, her eye focused on the floor. "It will not want to relinquish its foothold. It'll fight us every step of the way."

Closing her eyes, Tiqua began to chant—ancient words in a language that seemed to writhe and twist in the air, resonating with an eldritch power that set Kate's teeth on edge. The atmosphere in the room thickened, darkness pressing in at the edges of their small circle of candlelight, gravid with malice.

The Ouija board rattled, the planchette skittering across its surface like an insect in its death throes. Shadows danced along the walls, taking on monstrous shapes—grasping claws and gaping maws, empty eye sockets that wept black ichor. The cards glowed with an ethereal light, the intricate web they formed pulsing in response to Tiqua's incantations.

The room further darkened around them, shadows deepening and stretching, as if the very fabric of reality was bending to the will of the entity.

A high, chittering sound filled the air, the skittering of a thousand disembodied legs, the clack and rasp of something ancient and unspeakable dragging itself up from the abyss. Kate bit back a scream, terror a living thing trying to claw its way out of her chest.

In her mind's eye, an image slammed into her consciousness with the force of a wrecking ball—her parents, their faces contorted in unimaginable agony, wreathed in sickly orange-red flames. Their mouths gaped, charred lips peeling back from blackened gums as they reached for her, pleading, accusing. And beneath it all, threaded through each agonized cry, was a sibilant, gloating whisper...

They burn because of you, Kate. Because you abandoned them. Failed them. This is the fate you condemned them to...

Kate squeezed her eyes shut, tears tracking trails down her cheeks as she fought to banish the horrific vision, to remember it wasn't real, just another taunt from the sadistic entity trying to break her.

Beside her, James convulsed, a wounded sound tearing

from his throat. In his head, the staccato rattle of gunfire echoed, the stench of blood and fear as enemies swarmed from every direction. He watched, paralyzed, as his fellow soldiers fell one by one, their eyes accusing as the life drained from them.

Still just a scared little boy playing at war, a distorted version of his own voice sneered. *Did you think you could run from what you are? From the blood on your hands? There is no escape, James. Only an eternity in a hell of your own making...*

And at the center of it all, Tiqua writhed on the floor, back arching in agony as the demon assaulted her mind, digging up her deepest shame, her most secret guilt. Flashes of lives she couldn't save, wayward souls lost to the darkness because she wasn't strong enough, fast enough, good enough...

The malevolent laughter of the entity reverberated through the studio, a physical force that threatened to shatter bone and burst eardrums. It was feeding, glutting itself on their pain, savoring every delicious morsel of despair. Growing stronger. Hungrier.

With a strangled cry, Tiqua wrenched herself upright, scrabbling for the Ouija board with shaking hands. "Fight it!" she gasped, nails gouging bloody crescents into the planchette. "It's in your heads, using your own fears! Don't let it win!"

Kate and James clung to each other, anchoring themselves in the solidity of the other's presence. With a monumental effort, they shoved back against the deluge of nightmarish visions, focusing on Tiqua's desperate litany, on the fading hope that they could still somehow overcome this horror.

The planchette moved like a thing possessed, spelling out words in a frantic, jerky scrawl. O-N-E-B-Y-O-N-E-I-W-I-L-L-F-E-A-S-T

Tiqua snatched up the planchette with one trembling hand and slammed it back down onto the board. "By my blood, I consecrate this circle," she gritted out, nails gouging crimson crescents of beaded blood into her palms. "With my blood I consecrate this space! With my will I break your hold! What was sundered, let now be sealed!"

A blinding nova of light exploded from the cards, searing Kate's vision. The demon shrieked, high and agonized, its form shredding like mist beneath a punishing sun.

The cards of the spiral pattern flew into the air, whipping around the room in a razor-edged whirlwind. Tiqua ducked and wove through the maelstrom, teeth bared in a rictus of determination as her blood splattered the board, the howling vortex of energy building in the center of the room.

With a final, guttural cry, she slapped her palm flat against the planchette again, fingers splayed across the carved wood as if she could nail the portal shut through sheer force of will.

For a breathless, stretching second, the world hung suspended, the demon's roar rising to an earsplitting crescendo...and then, the shadows unraveled, the sickly metaphysical stench dissipating as the veil between worlds snapped closed with an almost audible crash.

In the sudden, yawning silence, the three of them knelt panting and wild-eyed. The Ouija board lay inert, the planchette just a harmless bit of wood in Tiqua's shaking hand. A litter of tarot cards fanned across the floor, their benevolent aura extinguished.

"Is it...is it gone?" Kate's voice shook, raw and threadbare.

Tiqua slumped back, a trickle of blood oozing from her left nostril. "For now," she rasped. "We hurt it. Severed its connection temporarily to this place, this plane."

She met their shell-shocked gazes, a hollow sort of victory in her eyes. "But it's not over. An entity that strong, that vicious...it won't give up. It will search for another way in. And when it finds one..."

She let the implication hang, heavy and rotten, in the charged air between them.

PART THREE

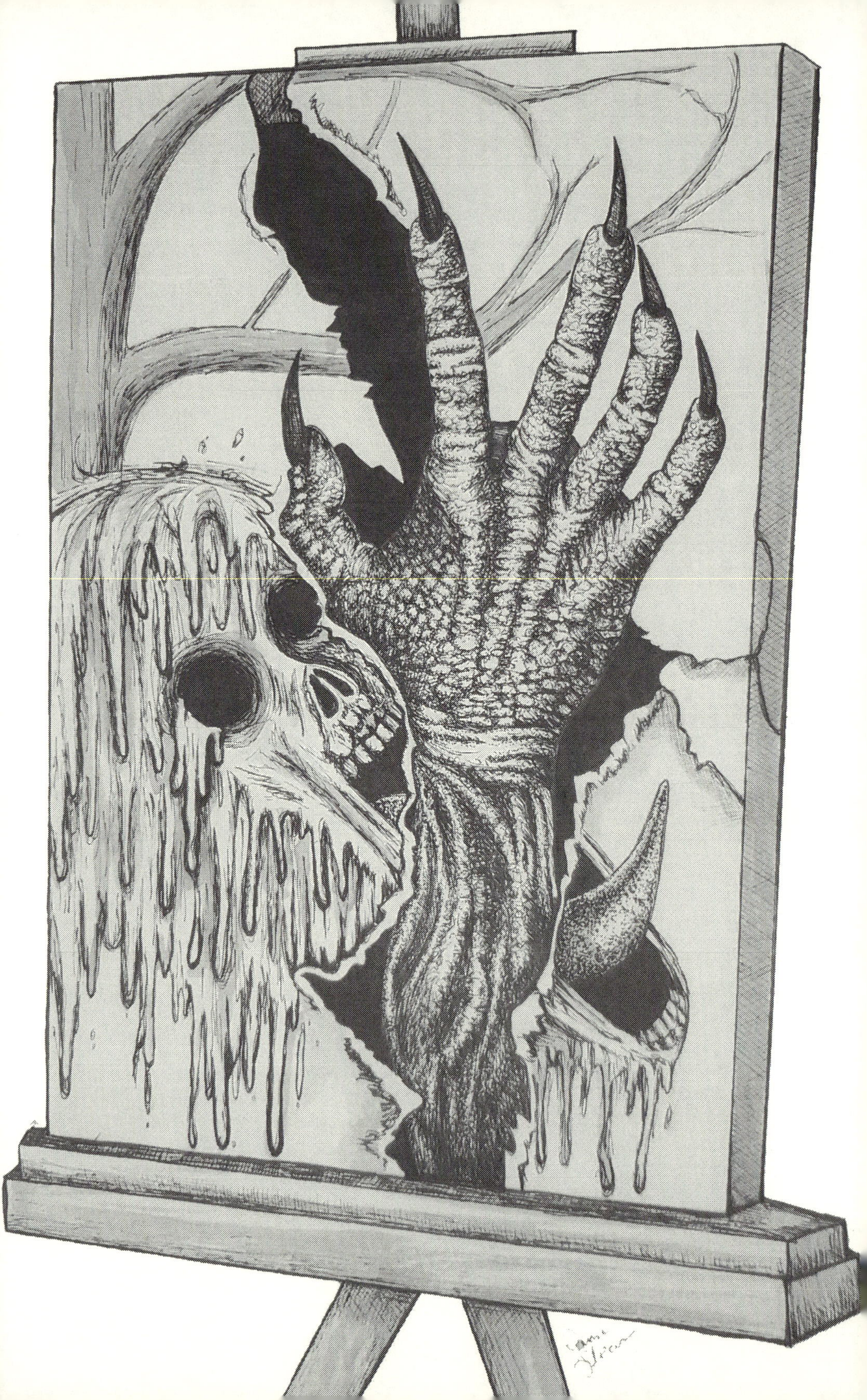

A PORTRAIT OF AGONY

Kate sat at the desk, shoulders slumped, feeling the effects of fatigue. Her eyes stung and a dull ache persisted in her temples from the prolonged lack of rest. Yet closing her eyes offered no respite from the nightmarish images that waited behind her lids, ready to pounce.

James ran a palm over his unshaven face, the weariness evident in his shadowed eyes that had seen too much. Perched on the corner of the desk with one foot braced against the floor for balance, he turned to the medium. "Where do we go from here, Tiqua? What's our next step?"

Tiqua lowered herself to the ground, folding her legs beneath her. She cradled her head in her palms as her fingers combed restlessly through her hair. Several long seconds passed without a sound while her slim shoulders shook almost imperceptibly. When at last she raised her head, her face was etched with hopelessness and resignation.

"The force we're up against is so much more powerful than anything I've faced before. My usual methods of protection and counteraction—the cards, rituals, and wards—they all feel so inadequate, like trying to hold back a raging storm with nothing more than flimsy paper. It's inevitable that these dark powers will overwhelm our defenses and break through, no matter what we do to stop them."

Kate's attention was drawn by a momentary movement at the periphery of her sight. Her head snapped up, a scream lodging in her throat as her gaze snagged on the painting and the entity with in it. Tall and emaciated, it seemed less a presence than an absence, a void that devoured the light and breathed shadows. It stared at her—*into her*—with a gaze like an open grave, and suddenly Kate was pinned, paralyzed, helpless even to blink as tears of blood beaded on her lashes and ice flooded her veins.

Distantly, she registered alarmed voices, hands on her shoulders shaking, shaking, but they belonged to another world, another life. Here, now, there was only the dark and the cold and the creeping, unspeakable awareness of the thing that had stolen her father and crouched now at the edges of her mind, waiting. Hungry.

"Kate? Kate!" Dimly, she registered Tiqua's voice, high and sharp with alarm.

With a shuddering gasp, the spell broke. Kate jackknifed forward, Tiqua's grip on her shoulders the only thing keeping her from crumpling to the floor. The shadows receded, but the tableau they left behind was its own breed of nightmare.

"The painting," she choked out, wild-eyed and panting.

James sprang to his feet. His face drained of color, eyes bulging as he stumbled back, one hand clasped to his mouth as if to physically hold back a scream.

Eleanor's portrait, once the featureless figure now horribly, grotesquely animated. It lurched toward them in violent, shuddering increments, the blank oval of its face bubbling, distorting, resolving into a death mask of agonized betrayal. Charred pits gaped where the eyes should be, the nose a skeletal ruin. The mouth stretched too wide, blackened gums peeling back from jagged teeth in a silent, endless scream.

And there, looming behind the ravaged specter of Kate's mother...the shadow man. It towered, wavered, a black pillar of pestilence and despair. Gangrenous fingers emerged from the folds of its rotting shroud, hovering above Eleanor's tortured face in a grotesque perversion of tenderness.

Kate could only stare, mute with atavistic horror, as the scene played out like some demented zoetrope. The colors of the painted background bled and ran, coalescing into new, terrible shapes—an endless expanse of blasted, colorless earth beneath a sky the color of old bruises. Forms moved in the poisoned mist beyond the edge of the frame, twisted and scuttling things her mind shied violently from identifying.

Tiqua was shouting now, the words lost beneath the roar of blood in Kate's ears, the juddering hammer of her heart. She felt the other woman's fingers dig into her arm, a bright point of pain in the numbing fog of terror.

"It's not her, Kate! That thing is corrupting your memories, using them to weaken you, to gain a foothold! Don't let it in!"

The sound of fabric tearing and splintering wood. The colorful background of acrylic paint was now a latticework of cracks. Reality unraveled before them, the boundaries between worlds stretching, distorting, tearing like rotten cloth. The thing clawed its way into being, a crude sketch of desiccated flesh and yellowed bone animated by unspeakable will and held together with pulsing ropes of shadow.

The frame buckled and warped as hands emerged from the edges of the canvas, skeletal and gnarled, the yellowed nails thick and curved like talons. It gripped the buckling frame, splinters flying as it pulled, heaving its grotesque body into view, splitting Eleanor's visage down the middle and the two halves of her painted form liquefied, spilling down off the canvas.

Kate couldn't move, couldn't scream. Her mind recoiled, rejecting the nightmare made manifest before her. The thing emerging from the painting was a twisted perversion of life, a crude assemblage of desiccated flesh and exposed bone held together by some unspeakable will. Its face was a ruin, a gaping hollow where features should be, empty sockets that burned with an infernal hunger.

"It's coming through!" Tiqua's scream was ragged, edged in hysteria. "We can't stop it, not here!"

The thing in the canvas shuddered, a grotesque parody of laughter bubbling from its ruined throat. With a sinuous grace that defied its decaying form, it unfolded itself from the shattered frame and began to climb, skeletal limbs scrabbling up the wall like a malformed spider. Empty sockets burned with a cold, covetous fire as it skittered down the wall, the wet rattle of its breath filling the room like a death rattle.

Tiqua was muttering now, a passage of words not meant for human mouths. Her nails scrabbled at the floorboards until they broke and bled, seeking...there. The planchette, edges digging into her palm as she thrust it toward Kate, her eyes black and fathomless.

"It's our only chance," she panted, wild-eyed and desperate. "We have to go through to the other side, fight it on its own ground. The portal works in both directions!"

Kate stared at the bit of thick wood and polished glass, uncomprehending.

Go through? Into the nightmare landscape of the painting that had birthed this abomination?

The idea was insanity, suicidal folly with a side of self-immolation. Every cell in her body screamed to run, to abandon this blighted house and its squirming shadows and never look back.

But...

Walter's face swam before her mind's eye, etched in lines of suffering and desolate resolve. He'd tried to warn her, even at the end. Tried to arm her for the battle to come, though he'd known it would likely be his last. She owed it to him to see this through, to finish what he'd started. Even if it damned her in the process.

Jaw clenched against the howl building in her throat, Kate gave a jerky nod, both women fiercely gripped the planchette until the wood bit into their skin, a blood oath etched in pain and determination. As one, they turned to face the nightmare that skittered down the wall, James a solid presence at their backs, his breath ragged with terror and grim resolve.

The wood of the frame gave an agonized groan as the creature hauled itself completely through the crumbling barrier between worlds, the reek of grave soil and rancid decay thickening the air. Kate gagged, her gorge rising, but she didn't flinch, didn't falter. Squaring her shoulders, she met Tiqua's gaze, finding her own resolve reflected back at her.

No words passed between them; none were needed. They knew the score, the stakes. Knew that wherever this macabre rabbit hole led, there would be no coming back from it, not really. Some doors, once opened, could never be fully closed again.

With a last, shuddering breath, they stepped forward as one, the planchette clutched between them like a talisman against the dark.

And as the shadows rushed up to claim them, as reality shredded and fell away, Kate's last coherent thought was a prayer, a desperate plea to any power that might be listening.

Let us be enough, she thought wildly, as the blackness swallowed her whole. *Please God, let us be enough.*

Then there was only the cold and the dark, and the screaming, the screaming, echoing in the abyss forever.

INTO THE ABYSS

T he world exploded.

Kate stood at the heart of a nightmarish hellscape, reality shattering and reforming around her in a kaleidoscope of impossible geometries and shrieking souls. Flames the color of infected wounds scoured the blasted landscape, whipping hungrily at the damned figures writhing in eternal torment. Above it all, a roiling sea of smoke-shadow boiled, shot through with veins of sullen, pulsating red.

And there, at the epicenter of the madness...Kate stood alone.

The realization slammed into her like a physical blow, driving the breath from her lungs in a ragged gasp. Mere moments ago, she and Tiqua had gripped the bloody planchette together, a lifeline against the encroaching darkness. But now, in the space between one blink and the next, Tiqua was simply...gone. Vanished, as if she had never been.

Panic surged through Kate's veins, a sickening tide of dread and disbelief. Her eyes darted wildly, desperately searching for any sign of her friend in the nightmare landscape.

"Tiqua!" she screamed, her voice swallowed by the cacophonous wails of the damned. "Tiqua, where are you?"

But there was no answer. No flash of recognition, no glimpse of Tiqua's familiar form amid the churning shadows. Only the unrelenting horror of this place, the bone-deep wrongness that permeated every molecule of the air.

Fear gnawed at her insides, but she forced herself to focus. Tiqua couldn't be gone. She couldn't have just disappeared into the ether, lost forever to this hellish realm. She had to be here somewhere, had to be fighting, searching for a way back to Kate's side.

Didn't she?

Gritting her teeth against the wail of hopelessness rising in her throat, Kate forced herself to move, to take one step after another across the shifting, undulating ground. Each footfall was an act of defiance, a refusal to succumb to the gibbering madness that pressed in on her from all sides.

"Tiqua!" she called again, desperation cracking the syllables into shards. "Tiqua, answer me!"

Silence, but for the ceaseless screams of the tortured and the wet, tearing sounds of things too terrible to name. The absence of her friend's voice, of the steadying anchor of her presence, was a yawning void in Kate's chest, a raw and bleeding wound.

She couldn't do this alone. Couldn't face the enormity of this place, the malevolent entity that had orchestrated their arrival, without Tiqua's quiet strength at her side. But what choice did she have? To surrender now, to let the darkness claim her without a fight...it would be a betrayal. Of Tiqua, of her father, of herself.

So she walked. Staggered and stumbled and clawed her way forward, even as the hellscape twisted and contorted around her, a living nightmare made manifest. The fetid air scraped her lungs raw, the stench of brimstone and charred flesh coating her tongue until she gagged on it. But still, she pressed on.

She had to find Tiqua. Had to end this, once and for all. For her father, for James, for the world she'd left behind.

There could be no other outcome. No other path but forward, into the heart of the abyss.

"I'm coming," she whispered, a vow and a prayer. "Tiqua, wherever you are...I'm coming for you."

As Kate ventured deeper into the surreal landscape, each step weighed heavy with uncertainty. The air crackled with despair, and the wails of tormented souls echoed through the twisted corridors of this nightmarish realm. With every passing moment, the oppressive atmosphere threatened to suffocate her resolve.

"Kate! Oh God, Katie, help us!"

A voice she knew down to the marrow of her bones, contorted almost beyond recognition by unfathomable agony.

Startled, she spun around, heart pounding in her chest. But it wasn't Tiqua's voice that called out to her. It was Walter's, his tone wrought with desperation and fear.

"Here! We're here, baby, please...it hurts, it hurts so much..."

"Dad?" The broken whisper scraped her throat raw, disbelief and wild, wretched hope conflicting in her chest. She spun in a frantic circle, squinting against the hellish glare, searching desperately for the source of that beloved voice. "Dad, where are you?"

There. Just ahead, wavering like a mirage in the shimmering heat. Two figures, hunched and clinging to each other, their forms twisted in impossible agony. Kate's heart stuttered, seized, then kicked into a staccato rhythm of sickening recognition.

"Mom? Dad!"

She lurched forward, staggering on numb legs, her arms outstretched in a wordless plea. Tears seared her cheeks, the salt of them mingling with the acrid tang of brimstone and despair. This couldn't be real, couldn't be happening...but her parents were there. Right there, close enough to touch if she could just move faster, reach further...

But with each stumbling step, the terrible truth became clearer, ripping a scream from Kate's raw and ruined throat. The figures before her were her parents...but not. Not anymore.

Their faces...dear God, their faces. Contorted into grotesque masks of torture, skin mottled and puckered where hellfire had seared the very flesh from their bones. Jaws cracked wide in permanent, silent screams, gaping maws lined with rows of needle-sharp teeth that gnashed and clacked in mindless anguish.

And their eyes...shit, their eyes. Bulging, writhing expanses of inky black shot through with pulsing veins of crimson and sickly yellow, the mad, unseeing gaze of the eternally damned.

Kate's gorge rose, her stomach clenching with a nausea too profound for retching. Every instinct screamed at her to run, to turn away from this twisted perversion of all she'd held dear. But her parents...

"Mom," she choked out, staggering ever closer despite the waves of wrongness radiating from their wasted forms. "Dad, I'm here. I'm here, just hold on..."

She stretched her fingers toward her mother's grasping, fleshless hand...only to jerk back with a shocked cry as blistering heat seared her skin. An invisible wall of pure, malicious energy crackled between her and her parents, the barrier rippling with the colors of an infected bruise.

"You cannot save them," the demon declared.

The voice seemed to come from everywhere and nowhere, a sepulchral growl that shook the very foundations of the hellscape. It reverberated in Kate's bones, in the bloody chambers of her pounding heart, inescapable and oppressive as the grave.

"No one can save them now...just as no one can save you."

Kate spun, scalded hand clutched to her chest, tears sizzling on her cheeks. There, coalescing from the billowing smoke and shadow...a figure. Towering, skeletal, its form a writhing mass of darkness shot through with veins of sulfurous yellow and pulsing, festering red.

A scream crawled up her throat, lodged there like a stone. It was the thing from the painting, the emaciated specter. But here, in this place between worlds...it was hideously, terribly real.

"You..." Kate managed, the word strangled and small. "What have you done to them? What have you done?!"

The thing laughed, a sound like the skittering of a thousand chitinous legs. "Me? Oh, my dear, sweet girl...I have merely shown them the truth of their existence. The agony that awaits all mortals in the end." Its lipless mouth stretched wide in a sharp-toothed parody of a grin. "Especially those foolish enough to summon me forth."

Kate shook her head mutely, denial and abject horror stealing her voice. This couldn't be happening. Couldn't be real. She was dreaming, hallucinating, had finally cracked under the strain of all she'd endured. She had to be.

"Their suffering is exquisite, is it not?" the demon purred, gliding closer in a sinuous ripple of shadow and flame. "Particularly your father. His soul was a rare delicacy as I devoured it, screaming, piece by quivering piece..."

"No!" The howl tore from Kate's throat, raw and ragged and bleeding. She lunged for the demon in a blind, hopeless fury, heedless of the searing barrier, the futility of her rage. Her hands blistered and blackened as they scrabbled uselessly at the crackling wall of energy, fresh agony swamping her senses. But it was nothing, less than nothing, compared to the fathomless anguish eviscerating her heart.

The demon laughed again, a skittering, chittering cackle of obscene delight. "Oh, that's precious. Such devotion! Such stubborn, stupid bravery!" It shook its grotesque head in mock admiration. "But I'm afraid your struggles are quite in vain. Your father is beyond saving now. Only the faintest echoes of his consciousness remain, and soon...even those will flicker out."

It leaned in, so close Kate could feel the putrid heat of its breath, could see the mad, swirling vortices of its eyes. When it spoke again, its voice was an insidious croon, honeyed poison dripping from every word.

"Of course, it needn't be a PERMANENT separation." Taloned fingers scraped Kate's tear-stained cheek, digging furrows of blood-edged ice in their wake. "I can be merciful. Benevolent, even. Give yourself to me willingly, and I will reunite you with your parents for all eternity."

A shudder of revulsion rippled through Kate, battling with the insidious temptation of the demon's promise. To see her parents again, hold them, even if only in an endless nightmare...for a moment, the desperate, broken thing keening in her chest yearned to accept. To surrender to the grotesqueries of this realm, to embrace oblivion, if only it meant an end to the yawning, empty ache of her grief.

And then she spoke.

THE DEVIL'S BARGAIN

"You can have me...in exchange for my father's soul," she said, her voice steady despite the gravity of her words. She met his gaze directly, unflinching.

The demon went preternaturally still, the shadows of its form pulsing with a new, ravenous intensity. "You would willingly serve yourself up to me?" it purred, a sickening undercurrent of glee threading through the words. "Lay yourself upon the altar of my hunger, condemn yourself to an eternity of torment...for him?"

Kate could only nod, not trusting herself to speak past the fear clawing at her throat, her heart, her very sanity. This was madness, a folly of the highest order...but what choice did she have? What sacrifice would be too great, if it meant freeing her father from this monster's clutches?

The demon drifted closer, the unreality of its form making her eyes water and her brain rebel. Up close, the darkness of it was dizzying, a physical weight pressing down on her until she feared her bones might splinter.

One emaciated hand extended, skeletal fingers unfurling like a fetid flower. Crooking in a beckoning gesture, a grotesque invitation.

"Then we have an accord," it hissed, hellfire eyes flaring with triumph.

And God help her...Kate reached back.

The moment their flesh met was an agony unlike any she had ever known, a pain that went beyond the physical, beyond thought and reason and self. It was the anguish of a soul being flayed apart, of a consciousness being unspooled like rotted thread.

But beneath the pain, beneath the all-consuming horror...a tiny, stubborn spark ignited in Kate's chest. A flicker of light in the endless dark, feeble but fierce.

The ember of an idea. The ghost of a plan.

Gritting her teeth against a scream, Kate let the weight of the demon's hunger pull her in, let its shadows enfold her. But even as its putrid essence began to leach into her skin, her bones, her secret, sorrowing heart...she dug deep. Deeper than fear, deeper than despair, deeper than the marrow and sinew of who she'd once been.

Down, down, down...to the very core of her, the bedrock foundation of Katherine Emerson. The part of her that was untouchable, inviolable, forged in the crucible of love and loss and sheer, stubborn will.

With a roar that shook the firmament of the infernal realm, Kate seized the demon's arm, her fingers sinking into the septic frailty of its form. It shrieked, a sound to shatter glass and splinter sanity, but she held fast. Held on with every last shred of strength and determination in her body.

And she began to pull.

In the studio, James and Tiqua stood frozen, staring in mute, slack-jawed horror at the scene unfolding before them within Walter's painting. At the chiaroscuro tableau of Kate, haloed in sickly orange light, grappling with a darkness so absolute it seemed to swallow the very air around them.

Her body was a livewire, a conduit for some unholy force that crackled along her nerve endings like static. Veins of inky black threaded through her pale skin, pulsing in time with the shuddering, skeletal frame of the entity she clung to.

"What do we do?" James croaked, feeling the hot sting of tears on his cheeks. "God, Tiqua, what do we do?"

But the other woman could only shake her head, her eyes wide and glassy with terror. "There's nothing we can do," she whispered, the words scraped raw. "This is...this is Kate's fight now. Her choice to make."

As if on cue, the demon loosed an unearthly howl, a sound that rattled James's teeth in his skull and sent every hair on his body standing at attention. It thrashed in Kate's grip, spasming and contorting, its hideous maw yawning wide as if to swallow her whole.

"No!" James screamed, lurching forward on instinct, on bone-deep denial. But an invisible force held him back, a wall of static and pressure that burned like frostbite. He could only watch, helpless and raging, as the woman he loved grappled with a monster now wearing her father's face. A truth so ugly it made his very soul cry out in revulsion.

And then, slowly, inexorably...the physical manifestation of the demon began to move. To slide across the floorboards like oil over water, dragged by the sheer force of Kate's will. Toward the painting, the portal, the crack between worlds that gaped like an open wound.

"She's doing it," Tiqua breathed, something like awe and

disbelief clashing in her voice. "God above, she's actually doing it. She's pulling the bastard back to hell."

But James couldn't share in her tentative hope, couldn't feel anything but the icy fist of dread around his hammering heart. Because he could see the toll it was taking on Kate, the price she was paying in blood and sanity. Could see the way the shadows crept higher, hungrier, staking their claim on her straining, sweat-slick form.

"The portal," he choked out, the words bitter as wormwood on his tongue. "If she pulls it all the way through, if she's still locked in that...that death-grip when it crosses over..."

He couldn't finish, couldn't voice the horrible truth searing behind his eyelids. Couldn't bear to imagine a world, a life, without the wild, reckless, stubborn magic of Kate Emerson blazing through it.

But he didn't need to say it aloud. Didn't need to spell out the inevitability they could all taste on the air like ozone, like rot. The terrible, inescapable reality that was barreling toward them with all the mercy of a freight train.

In the space between one heartbeat and the next, Kate would have a choice to make.

A sacrifice.

Because to unchain Walter's soul from the demon's fetid grip, to cast the entity back into the abyss and seal the breach behind it...she would have to relinquish her own. Surrender herself to the hungry dark, sever the gossamer tether binding her to this plane and to the ones she loved beyond reason.

Something in James shattered at the knowledge, a fault line spiderwebbing through the very bedrock of his being. This couldn't be happening. He couldn't lose her, not like this, not when they'd only just begun to find their way back to each other. There had to be another way, a loophole, a Hail Mary play to undo this devil's bargain.

But deep down, in the secret, howling place he scarcely dared to venture...he knew there wasn't. Knew it with a certainty that settled in his bones like permafrost, cold and inexorable.

Kate Emerson would martyr herself on the altar of her love for her father. For the tattered remnants of their broken family.

She would pay the ultimate price...and James would spend the rest of his life trying to fill the void she left behind.

Inside the infernal realm of Walter's creation, the demon bucked and writhed, its fetid essence boiling with rage and hunger. But Kate held fast, feeling her muscles scream and her tendons pop, channeling every last ounce of strength into her grip.

"You can't have him!" she snarled, spitting the words

through bared teeth. "You can't have any of them! I won't let you!"

The demon shrieked, an ungodly sound, and redoubled its efforts to throw her off. Its claws raked down her arms, shredding fabric and flesh alike, painting the air with arcs of crimson. But the pain was distant, unimportant. Subsumed beneath the enormity of her purpose, the blinding purity of her love.

TIQUA'S GAMBIT

Tiqua knelt on the floor of the studio, her face a mask of desperate focus as she shuffled the worn tarot deck with trembling hands. The air was thick with the stench of brimstone and putrefaction, the oppressive weight of the entity's malevolence bearing down like a physical thing.

"Kate!" she cried, her voice raw with urgency. "I need you to hold it off, just for a little longer. I think...I think I know how we can stop it, but I need time."

Across the divide of worlds, Kate battled the nightmare made flesh—a towering figure of shadow and rot, its emaciated limbs twisting at impossible angles, its gaping maw dripping with an ichor that sizzled where it hit the floor. The thing that had once been trapped within the painting, clawing its way into their world with a hunger that defied comprehension.

Tiqua's jaw clenched, a muscle ticking beneath the rich umber of her skin. "You can do this, Kate. You have to. Your father, James, me...we're all counting on you. Dig deep, find that spark of light inside you and hold onto it. Don't let this thing snuff it out!"

Kate shuddered, nausea churning in her gut as the entity's shadows lapped at her feet like eager dogs. But beneath the fear, beneath the soul-deep horror...she felt it. That ember of determination, of love and grief and raging, defiant hope. With a scream that bordered on feral, she flung her hands out before her, a barrier of pure, blazing will slamming into place between her and the advancing darkness.

The creature recoiled with a hiss, its form rippling and contorting in a grotesque mockery of pain. But it didn't retreat, didn't release its hold on this world. Instead, it seemed to swell, to grow, its darkness pulsing like a rotten heart.

Around her, swelling from the fiery brimstone and sulfur,

emanating from the superheated air, Kate could hear Tiqua chanting under her breath, the ancient words thrumming with power. The tarot cards flashed between her fingers, a blur of arcane symbols and faded colors as she laid them out in a complex pattern around the edges of the mutilated painting—a mandala of might, a spiritual conduit for the forces she sought to wield.

Each card placed sent a jolt through Kate's body, a surge of heat and light that raced along her nerve endings like liquid fire. It was agony and ecstasy twined, a searing, transcendent pain that threatened to strip her mind raw. But with each fresh wave, she felt her own strength grow, her will crystallizing into a brilliance that scorched the eyes and set the teeth on edge.

The entity screamed, a sound like nails on a chalkboard amplified to eardrum-rupturing proportions. It lunged for her, talons extended, slavering jaws yawning wide—a black hole, an abyss made of hunger and hate. Kate met it head-on, her own scream rising to meet it, pouring every ounce of her grief and rage and love into the maelstrom between them.

Light and shadow crashed together, a cataclysm in miniature that sent shockwaves rippling through the fabric of reality. The creature writhed, its form shredding at the edges as Kate's power, backed by Tiqua's ritual, tore through it like a thousand razored teeth. Gobbets of stinking, tarry flesh spattered the canvas, the floor, the ceiling—a visceral Jackson Pollock of gore and corruption.

And through it all, Tiqua's chanting grew—a rhythmic pulse, an insistent drumbeat that wove itself through the chaos and drew it tight. The tarot cards flared with eldritch light, burning away the lingering shadows, cauterizing the wound in the world that the entity had forced its way through.

With a final, glass-shattering howl, the creature imploded—a singularity of darkness collapsing in on itself, devouring its own essence in a self-annihilating frenzy. The shock of its banishment sent Kate staggering, her knees buckling as the adrenaline and borrowed power drained from her in a rush.

But before she could hit the ground, translucent arms caught her—achingly familiar, infinitely precious. Heart in her throat, Kate looked up into the shimmering, spectral face of her father.

No longer ravaged by sickness and despair, Walter's features were suffused with a peace she'd never seen on him in life. Tears of light tracked down his cheeks as he cradled her close, his touch a whisper of coolness against her fever-bright skin.

"Katie," he murmured, his voice a wonder. "My brave, brilliant girl. I'm so proud of you. So grateful."

Kate's own tears spilled over, carving channels through the ash and ichor streaking her skin. "Daddy," she choked out. "I'm sorry, I'm so sorry. I should have been there, should have..."

But Walter was already shaking his head, a finger pressing gently against her lips. "No, sweetheart. You have nothing to apologize for. You saved me—saved all of us. You faced down the darkness and you won."

He smiled, a radiant, joyful thing. "I'm free now, Katie-girl. Free in a way I haven't been since...since your mama left us. And that's because of you. Because of your strength, your love."

Kate's heart seized, a sweet, piercing ache. "I miss you," she whispered, raising a hand to trace the contours of his ghostly cheek. "I don't...I don't know how to do this without you."

"You'll learn," Walter promised. "You'll grieve and you'll heal and you'll grow. And when you need me, when the weight of memory grows too heavy...I'll be here. Watching over you, until it's time to meet again on the other side."

He was growing fainter now, his form beginning to blur at the edges. Kate clutched at him, a sob tearing its way free of her throat. "Dad, wait..."

"I love you, Katie." His voice was an echo, a sigh on the breeze. "Always and forever. Be brave, be bold...but above all, be happy. That's all I've ever wanted for you."

And with a final flare of light, a last brush of phantasmal fingers against her tear-streaked face...he was gone.

The world tilted, a sickening lurch that sent Kate's stomach heaving. Through the haze of exhaustion and soul-deep grief, she was dimly aware of hands on her shoulders, reaching through the frame of unreality, of James's stricken face looming over her, his lips forming words she couldn't make out over the roaring in her ears.

Then, between one blink and the next, the floor opened beneath her—a yawning chasm that reeked of fire and despair. The infernal realm, the nightmare dimension the entity had clawed its way out of...and now, in her weakened state, it sought to draw her down into its fetid embrace.

Distantly, she heard Tiqua scream her name, felt the crackle of ancient energy as the other woman tried frantically to weave a net of power to catch her. But it was too little, too late. The abyss had her, and it would not let go.

As the darkness swallowed her whole, as the sulfurous winds tore at her hair and clothes and the distant shrieks of damned souls filled her ears...Kate's last thought was a prayer. Not for herself, but for those she left behind.

"Keep them safe," she whispered into the void, a final, fervent plea.

Then the blackness took her.

THE RABBIT HOLE'S END

Kate's body was seized by a relentless descent, a dizzying tumble into a seemingly infinite chasm of swirling darkness. The air grew cold, biting at her skin as she fought to orient herself in the disorienting gloom. A strangled cry escaped her lips, but it was quickly smothered by the suffocating silence of the abyss, a void that devoured sound and light, leaving only a chilling sense of isolation and impending doom.

From a distance, the frantic sound of James calling her name barely reached her ears, his voice hoarse and strained with fear. The rhythmic cadence of Tiqua's chant, filled with words she couldn't understand, pulsed in the air. An acrid, electric energy crackled and intensified as the medium focused every bit of their strength on the struggle.

Senses were dulled, distorted, as if shrouded in a suffocating fog of pain and fear. The emptiness pressed in, a nauseating weight filling Kate's nose and mouth, leaving the metallic taste of decay on her tongue and throat. It seeped into her lungs, a viscous, smothering oil that saturated every fiber of her being until she felt more shadow than flesh, a hollow shell for its vile essence.

Kate's body twisted uncontrollably, her muscles contracting and distorting her limbs into unnatural positions as the encroaching darkness filled the voids within her. It felt as if she was disintegrating, her identity unraveling like a decaying thread. The boundaries of her mind blurred and dissolved, fragments of memories, thoughts, and her very being dissolving into the relentless abyss.

And still she fell, unabated, a relentless plummet. Time twisted around her, each moment an eternity, each eternity a fleeting breath. The darkness enveloped her, a suffocating void that whispered promises of oblivion, its insidious tendrils creeping into her consciousness with a chilling touch.

Give in... it crooned, the tone a grotesque echo of enticement.

...Release your hold. This is your ordained path, your inheritance. Your very essence was crafted for dissolution, to fragment and disperse upon the unforgiving maw of nothingness...

Silent tears tracked through the dust on Kate's face. A desperate cry for release echoed in the hollow of her mind, but her lips remained immobile.

There was no way out, no reprieve, no finality. Only the ceaseless, suffocating weight of existence and the insidious allure of a transformation she dreaded. Yet, a treacherous voice whispered...

...Why resist? You can finally rest. There is no more pain...

Surrender beckoned, promising oblivion.

...give in...

In the midst of turmoil, a faint spark ignited, defying the surrounding darkness.

...let me fill all your broken places...

A fragile glimmer persisted against the immense, encroaching darkness.

... you'll never feel anything ever again...

It pierced the fog of Kate's stupor, pulling her back from the edge of oblivion. It was a jarring sensation, an abrupt intrusion that sent a shiver of awareness down her spine and reignited her senses.

Light.

Within the boundless abyss of night, a pinprick of luminescence flickered. Ephemeral and trembling, yet stubbornly persistent. A lone candle's flame defied the darkness, a fragile bulwark against a sky barren of celestial bodies and devoid of the promise of daybreak.

Kate kicked out with what remained of her strength, floundering and graceless. Straining for that fragile glow with everything in her, every stubborn scrap of will and defiance. The void shrieked, a sound to chill the marrow, and redoubled its efforts to drag her under. To douse that thimbleful of brightness in an ocean of shadow.

But still, Kate fought. Clawing and thrashing, hauling herself hand over hand through the morass of despair. Fixing her eyes on the light and refusing to look away, even as the void raked her raw and scoured her to the bone.

Closer now, close enough to recognize the shape of it, revealing the familiar silhouette. Tiqua's wards sparked to life, their protective energy surging with the medium's dwindling strength. A powerful arm, adorned with a glowing golden sigil that seemed to pulse in time with a living heart, flexed and coiled in anticipation.

James.

With a surge of desperation, reaching for her, straining across the impossible chasm between them. His hand outstretched, grasping, a lifeline thrown into the churning sea of Kate's damnation.

A desperate sound escaped her lips as she surged forward into the darkness. Her body ached with longing, her mind fixated on the single, overwhelming desire to bridge the distance between them, to entwine her fingers with his and find solace in an embrace that would never end.

Contact.

A spark, a frisson, a circuit completing with a snap of ozone and a crackle of power. James's hand locked around Kate's wrist, solid and searing, anchor against the overwhelming force threatening to pull her away. With a roar of effort and a blaze of light, he heaved backward, hauling her up and out with a strength borne of love and terror in equal measure.

The void shrieked, a sound like all the fury and anguish of hell distilled into a single, skin-flaying keen. Its talons raked Kate as she tore free of its embrace, leaving great weeping gashes that ran soul-deep. But James's grip never faltered, his hold on her an unbreakable tether, and with a final, wrenching surge, she burst through the surface of the nightmare—

—and tumbled onto the floor of the studio, a tangle of limbs and labored breath and the salt-sting of tears. Kate landed atop James with a graceless "oof", every nerve ending screaming as sensation came flooding back in a tidal wave. She was shaking violently, the shocked, full-body jitters of a person wrenched back from the very brink of annihilation.

Dimly, she registered Tiqua slumping back against the wall, the glow of the wards guttering out around her like spent candles. Heard the medium's hitching, relief-soaked sobs, muffled behind the hands she'd clasped over her mouth. Felt the thrum of James's pulse beneath her cheek, the heaving rise and fall of his chest as he struggled to master himself.

But loudest of all was the sudden, echoing silence in her own mind. The yawning absence where the void's insidious whispers had burrowed and bred, a parasitic infestation metastasizing through her gray matter. It was gone, scoured away by the cleansing fire of the wards and James's sheer, bullheaded refusal to let her go.

Leaving behind a lightness, a clarity of being, that Kate hadn't known since...God, since before her mother's death. Since the first chilly tendrils of grief and helplessness had twined around her heart and began to squeeze.

A broken sound hitched in her throat, halfway between a laugh and a sob. She pushed up on trembling arms, just far enough to meet James's gaze. To drink in the sight of his beloved face, drawn and haggard but so beautifully, gloriously alive.

"Is it...?" She couldn't finish, the words clogging in her raw and ravaged throat. But James understood, his hands coming up to cradle her tear-stained cheeks with a tenderness that made fresh moisture well and spill.

"It's over," he rasped, wonder and disbelief and bone-deep exhaustion thrumming through the words. "It's done, Kate. We did it. You...Christ, you brilliant, brave, impossible girl. You beat it."

A shudder rippled through her, the adrenaline-soaked tension of the last harrowing minutes (hours, days, a lifetime?) draining out of her all at once and leaving behind a numb, leaden sort of lassitude. She collapsed against James's chest with a whimper, limbs gone watery. Let herself be gathered up and held, his arms locking around her like steel bands as he rocked her gently.

Over the thunder of her own pulse, she could make out Tiqua murmuring in the foreign tongue—a purifying ritual, a blessing, a salve to soothe the frayed edges of her nascent soul. The air tasted different, smelled different. Charged and prickling but clean, untainted by the oily residue of the beast's malice.

Slowly, Kate wrenched her head up, eyes seeking out the easel. The canvas lay placid and unmolested, the lurid gash knitted shut as if it had never been. Just cracked paint and drying oils, pigment and primer and not a single whiff of infernal corruption.

"Will it stay gone?" she asked, the words thin and thready in the hush. "We didn't...didn't banish it or exorcise it or whatever it is you're supposed to do with demons. We just closed the door it came through."

"And sealed it," Tiqua replied, her voice raw but ringing with conviction. "That's the thing about doors, Kate. They can be locked. Barred. Warded against entry from either side." She scrubbed a still-shaking hand over her ashen face, a grim smile touching her lips. "With the portal closed and my shields in place...that thing won't be darkening your doorstep again. Not in this world or the next."

A beat, the words sinking in. Then James was letting out a whoop of mingled jubilation and relief, crushing Kate against his chest and burying his face in the sweat-soaked tangle of her hair. She clung to him just as fiercely, fresh tears streaking her cheeks as the reality of it crashed over her in a wave.

It was over. The nightmare, the horror, the choking pall of evil that had haunted her every waking moment since that first terrible night...all of it, vanquished in a blaze of light and the unflinching grip of the bonds she'd forged. The shattered remnants of her family could rest now. Walter and Eleanor, reunited at last in whatever waited beyond the veil.

And Kate...for the first time in longer than she could remember, Kate could breathe again.

Oh, she was under no illusions that the road ahead would be easy. Trauma of this magnitude left scars, fault lines scored deep into the bedrock of a person's psyche. She had no doubt that there would be nightmares, flashbacks, moments when the darkness felt like it was rushing back in to swallow her whole.

But she wasn't alone anymore. Her gaze rose to find James watching her, pride and tenderness and something deeper, something brighter, limning every beloved plane and angle of his face. To Tiqua, wan but smiling, the clean-scoured brilliance of her aura chasing away the last lingering shadows.

No, Kate wasn't alone. And with these two at her side—

her shield-mate, her ward-worker, the makeshift family she'd forged in the crucible of shared horror and hard-won survival...

She knew they could weather any storm. Knew it down to her bones, with a certainty as solid and unshakable as bedrock. The memories, the scars, might never fully fade. But they would walk it together, hand in hand and heart to heart. They would claw their way back to the light, no matter how dark the path grew.

And heaven help any force, earthly or otherwise, that tried to stand in their way.

EPILOGUE

Three weeks passed in a numbing montage of sympathy cards, legal documents, and the dreary administrative tasks involved in settling Walter's estate. Kate drifted through it all in a haze, her grief a persistent undercurrent that colored her thoughts and tugged at her emotions, day and night.

But today...today was the final hurdle. The last bit of business to be handled before she could close the book on this chapter of her life and try to find her way forward in a world upended.

She stood in the center of the living room, watching as the Goodwill workers carried out the last of Walter's belongings. Furniture that had once held family gatherings, knick-knacks that had adorned shelves and told stories, the assorted objects that accumulate over a lifetime, all of it was now carefully packed into the truck, soon to be scattered to new homes.

The house felt unfamiliar in its emptiness, the absence of personal touches leaving a silence where laughter and conversation had once filled the air.

But there was one thing left. One final, unavoidable task that Kate had been putting off, dreading with every fiber of her being.

Walter's painting.

It still sat in the studio, propped on the easel like taunt, a dare, a silent challenge to the forces of darkness that had tried so hard to claim her.

With a subtle lift of her chin, Kate ascended the staircase, her footsteps steady against the quiet urge to retreat. At Walter's studio door, her fingers hesitated on the cool metal of the knob. She paused a moment before drawing in a deep breath and stepping inside.

The familiar room held the same lingering aroma of turpentine, yet now an underlying, vaguely unpleasant odor

THE DEVIL'S DOORWAY

permeated the air, hinting at something stale or decaying hidden from view. In the middle of this unsettling atmosphere, the painting commanded attention.

Under the dim light, the painting appeared to throb subtly, its hues undulating and morphing in an unsettling display. The repaired tear in the canvas, a vestige of the harrowing encounter, created an illusion of respiration, a subtle rise and fall against the wall.

"You don't get to win," she whispered, a raspy thread of sound caught in the dryness of her throat. "Do you hear me? I won't let you. I won't."

But even as she spoke, Kate felt it, the insidious, growing discordance of the lurking just beyond the veil. Biding its time, gathering its strength for another assault on the fragile boundaries between worlds.

The quiet sound of a step behind her shattered the heavy silence. Kate whirled around, her heart pounding in her chest. Relief washed over her as she saw James. His brow was furrowed with worry as he observed her stiff stance and the way her hands were clenched tightly at her sides.

"The truck's all loaded up," he said quietly, coming to stand beside her. His gaze flicked to the painting, something hard and fierce kindling in the depths of his eyes. "Is that...?"

"The last thing," Kate confirmed.

James blew out a slow breath, rubbing a hand across his chin. "Christ. What are we going to do with it? We can't just...I don't know, toss it in the donation pile with the rest of Walter's things."

"I know." Kate's throat worked as she swallowed, her nails biting into her palms. "Believe me, I know."

The urge to destroy, to obliterate the canvas filled her, an insatiable need to rip and tear and shred until nothing remained but shreds of canvas and the haunting memories. Better still, to set it ablaze, reducing it to cinders that would scatter to the distant corners of the earth on the breeze.

But Tiqua's warning whispered in her mind...

Destroying the painting might sever its connection to this world...but it could also break the seals. Shattering the barrier holding the darkness at bay could unleash hell on earth, with no way to stop it.

"We can't risk it," she said aloud, the words bitter as wormwood on her tongue. "Tiqua said she'd take it. Keep it safe, ward it with every protection her family knows. Lock it down so tight that nothing could ever slip through again."

James's jaw clenched, a muscle ticking in his cheek. For a moment, she thought he might argue, might demand a more proactive solution. But then his shoulders slumped, a heavy sigh gusting from his lungs.

"You're right," he admitted, sounding as tired and worn thin as Kate felt. "We have to trust her. Trust that she knows what she's doing."

Kate nodded, tearing her gaze away from the painting

with an almost physical effort. Outside, a horn honked—the Goodwill truck, impatient to be on its way.

"I guess that's our cue," James said, attempting a smile that didn't quite reach his eyes. "You ready to get out of here?"

"God, yes," Kate breathed, the words fervent and heartfelt. "Let's go."

Together, they made their way downstairs and out into the crisp autumn air. The sun was warm on Kate's face, the breeze fresh and clean after the oppressive staleness of the house. For a moment, she just stood there, tilting her head back and breathing deep. Letting the light and the sky and the sheer, unrelenting normalcy of the day wash over her.

Beside her, James was silent, his shoulder brushing hers as they watched the Goodwill truck rumble away down the street. And then it was just the two of them, standing in front of the house that had held a lifetime of memories, good and bad, cherished and cursed.

Kate's gaze fell on the "For Sale" sign stuck in the front lawn, its bright red letters garish against the grass.

Another ending, another chapter closed.

The thought brought a fresh wave of grief, sharp and sudden as a punch to the solar plexus.

"So," James said softly, breaking the hush that had fallen. "What now?" When she glanced at him, he elaborated, something tentative and almost shy in his expression. "Are you...will you go back to LA? Pick up your life where you left off?"

Kate hesitated, worrying her lower lip between her teeth. It was the question she'd been avoiding, the decision she'd been putting off in the face of more immediate concerns. But now, with Walter buried and the house emptied and the evil laid to rest...she couldn't dodge it any longer.

LA.

Her job, her friends, her carefully cultivated existence a world away from the grief and the horror that had consumed her here. It would be so easy to slip back into that life, to let the bustle and the distance and the sheer, relentless forward momentum of it all dull the edges of her loss. To pack this whole nightmare away in a box labeled "Do Not Open" and shove it to the darkest corners of her psyche.

But even as the thought crossed her mind, Kate knew it for the lie it was. There was no going back, no unseeing the things she'd witnessed or unknowing the terrible truths she'd learned. The darkness that had touched her, the evil that had sunk its claws into her very soul...it would follow her, no matter how far or fast she ran.

And more than that...there were other ties, other bonds holding her to this place. To the city that had forged her, the memories both painful and precious. To the man standing at her side, the one who'd been her rock, her anchor, her north star through the worst storm of her life.

James, who looked at her now with such open understanding, such quiet acceptance. Waiting patiently for her answer, for her choice, even if it shattered his own heart in the process.

Slowly, carefully, Kate reached out and twined her fingers with his. Met his startled gaze with her own, clear and steady for the first time in what felt like forever.

She didn't know what came next. Didn't know what fresh horrors might be waiting in the wings, what new battles they might be called to fight. But she knew, with a bone-deep certainty, that she wouldn't face them alone. That the man beside her and the history they shared, was worth fighting for. Worth building a new life, a new beginning, from the ashes of the old.

ABOUT THE AUTHOR

Steven Pajak, a Chicago-based author, crafts stories that explore the depths of horror and the human psyche. With a pen that dances on the edges of darkness, Steven brings to life tales that challenge, terrify, and linger in the minds of readers. Drawing inspiration from the urban tapestry of Chicago, his work merges the pulse of city life with the eerie quiet of the shadows lurking within the darkest corners of our minds. Steven invites you into a world where fear meets courage, and the journey through his imagination proves as haunting as it is unforgettable.

- facebook.com/StevenPajakAuthor
- instagram.com/stevenpajak_official
- amazon.com/author/stevenpajak
- goodreads.com/stevenpajakauthor

Also by Steven Pajak

Novels

Darkness Within

Project Hindsight

The Haunting of Elena Vera

The Devil's Doorway

Murder, Inc.

The Mad Swine Trilogy

The Fallen

Dead Winter

New Dawn

U.S. Marshal Jack Monroe Series

Wolves Among Sheep

Nowhere to Run

Collections

Dark Days: Novellas of Revenge and Redemption